ST. MARTIN'S

MINOTAUR

MYSTERIES

Hardcase

DAN SIMMONS

St. Martin's Paperbacks

HARDCASE

Copyright © 2001 by Dan Simmons.
Excerpt from *Hard Freeze* © 2002 by Dan Simmons.

Cover photo © David Job / Stone

Library of Congress Catalog Card Number: 2001019165

ISBN: 0-312-98016-7

Printed in the United States of America

St. Martin's Press hardcover edition / July 2001
St. Martin's Paperbacks edition / August 2002

St. Martin's Paperbacks are published by St. Martin's Press, 175 Fifth
Avenue, New York, NY 10010.

10   9   8   7   6   5   4   3   2

This book is for Richard Stark, who sometimes writes under the wussy pseudonym of Donald Westlake.

Hardcase

CHAPTER 1

Late one Tuesday afternoon, Joe Kurtz rapped on Eddie Falco's apartment door.

"Who's there?" Eddie called from just the other side of the door.

Kurtz stood away from the door and said something in an agitated but unintelligible mumble.

"What?" called Eddie. "I said who the fuck's there?"

Kurtz made the same urgent mumbling noises.

"Shit," said Eddie and undid the police lock, a pistol in his right hand, opening the door a crack but keeping it chained.

Kurtz kicked the door in, ripping the chain lock out of the wood, and kept moving, shoving Eddie Falco deeper into the room. Eddie was several inches taller and at least thirty pounds heavier than Kurtz, but Kurtz had momentum on his side.

Eddie swung down the 9mm Browning. Still shoving the taller man across the floor and into the wooden blinds on the window side of the apartment, Kurtz had his arm blocked across Eddie's chest, his right hand squeezing the base of the man's upper bicep. He quickly slid his left hand across the top of the Browning.

Eddie squeezed the trigger. Just as Kurtz had planned, the hammer fell on the webbing between the thumb and forefinger of Kurtz's hand.

Kurtz took the weapon away from Eddie and backhanded him into the wall.

"Fucking sonofabitch!" yelled Eddie, rubbing blood off his face. "You broke my goddamn—" Eddie made a lunge for the pistol.

Kurtz tossed the Browning out the open sixth-floor window, held Eddie off with his left arm, and kicked the other man's legs out from under him. Eddie's head hit the hardwood floor with a bang. Kurtz knelt on his chest.

"Tell me about Sam," said Kurtz.

"Who the fuck is . . ." gasped Eddie Falco.

"Samantha Fielding," said Kurtz. "The redhead that you killed."

"Redhead?" said Eddie, spitting blood. "I didn't know the bitch's name, I just—"

Kurtz put all of his weight on one knee and Eddie's eyes bugged out. Then Kurtz held his left hand palm out, jabbed hard, and flattened Eddie's broken nose against the screaming man's cheek. "Talk nice," he said. "She worked with me."

Eddie's face was alternating chalk white and dark red under the blood. "Can't breathe," he gasped. "Get . . . off . . . please."

Kurtz stood.

Eddie gasped some more, spat blood, got to one knee slowly, and then threw himself through the kitchen door.

Kurtz followed him into the tiny kitchen.

Eddie swung around with a butcher knife. He crouched, feinted, lunged, and then seemed to levitate up and back as Kurtz place-kicked him in the balls. Eddie came down hard on a counter filled with unwashed dishes. He was gasping and retching while he rolled, smashing soiled dishes under him.

Kurtz took the knife and threw it at the far wall, where it stuck and vibrated like a tuning fork.

"Sam," said Kurtz. "Tell me about what happened the night you killed her."

Eddie lifted his head and squinted at Kurtz. "Fuck you!" He grabbed another, shorter kitchen knife from the countertop.

Kurtz sighed, forearmed the thug in the throat, bent him back over the sink, and jammed Eddie's right hand down deep into the garbage disposal. Eddie Falco was screaming even before Kurtz reached over and turned on the switch.

Kurtz gave it thirty seconds and then shut off the disposal, ripped Eddie's bloody undershirt down the front, and wrapped the rag around the stumps of the man's fingers. Eddie's face was now pure white under a spattering of blood. His mouth was open and his eyes were protruding as he stared at what was left of his hand. Someone began pounding on the wall from the apartment next door.

"Help! Murder!" screamed Eddie. "Somebody call the cops! Help!"

Kurtz let him scream for a few seconds and then dragged him back into the main room and dropped him into a chair next to the table. The pounding on the wall had stopped, but Kurtz could hear shouts from the neighbors.

"The cops are coming," gasped Eddie Falco. "The cops'll be here in a minute."

"Tell me about Sam," Kurtz said softly.

Eddie clutched the bloody rag around his hand, glanced toward the open window as if expecting sirens, and licked his lips. He mumbled something.

Kurtz gave him a hearty handshake. This time, the screaming was so loud that even the neighbors fell silent.

"Sam," said Kurtz.

"She found out about the coke deal when she was looking for that runaway brat." Eddie's voice was a gagging monotone. "I didn't even know her fucking name." He looked up at Kurtz. "It wasn't me, you know. It was Levine."

"Levine said it was you."

Eddie's eyes flickered back and forth. "He's lying. Get him in here and ask him. He killed her. I just waited in the car."

"Levine isn't around anymore," said Kurtz, his tone

conversational. "Did you rape her before you cut her throat?"

"I tell you it wasn't me. It was that goddamn Le—" Eddie started screaming again.

Kurtz released the shapeless pulp that had been Eddie Falco's nose. "Did you rape her first?"

"Yeah." Something like defiance flickered in Eddie's eyes. "Fucking cunt put up a fight, tried to—"

"Okay," said Kurtz, patting Eddie on his bloody shoulder. "We're about done."

"Whaddaya mean?" The defiance turned to terror.

"I mean the cops will be here in a minute. Anything else you want to tell me?"

Sirens wailed. Eddie lunged to his feet and staggered toward the open window as if to scream at the cops to hurry, but Kurtz slammed him against the wall and held him in place with a forearm hard against his chest. Eddie squirmed and struck at Kurtz with his left hand and the ruins of his right fist. Kurtz ignored him.

"I swear I didn't—"

"Shut up," explained Kurtz. He grabbed the bigger man by what was left of his shirtfront and dragged him closer to the window.

"You're not going to kill me," said Eddie.

"No?"

"No," Eddie twitched his head in the direction of the window just inches away. Six stories below, two police cruisers had slid to a stop. Neighbors were broiling out of the apartment building, pointing toward the window. One of the cops drew his gun as he saw Kurtz and Eddie. "They'd send you away forever!" gasped Eddie, his breath hot and rank in Kurtz's face.

"I'm not that old," said Kurtz. "I have some years to spare."

Eddie lunged away, ripping what was left of the rags of his shirt, stood in the open window and waved and screamed at the cops below. "Hurry! For fuck's sake, hurry!"

"You in a hurry?" said Kurtz. "Here." He grabbed Eddie Falco by his hair and the seat of his pants and threw him out the open window.

Neighbors and cops scattered. Eddie screamed all the way down to the roof of the closest police cruiser. Pieces of chrome and glass and Plexiglas from the gumball-flasher array on the top of the cruiser flew in all directions after Eddie hit.

Three of the cops ran into the building with their weapons raised.

Kurtz stood silent for a second and then went over to open the door wider. He was on his knees in the center of the room with his fingers linked behind his head when the cops burst in a moment later.

CHAPTER 2

In the old days, they would have opened the front man-door for Kurtz and let him leave wearing a cheap new suit, with his possessions in a brown paper bag. These days they provided him a cheap vinyl bag for his possessions and gave him chinos, a blue button-down shirt, an Eddie Bauer windbreaker, and a bus ride into nearby Batavia.

Arlene Demarco picked him up at the bus station. They drove north to the Thruway and then west in silence.

"Well," Arlene said at last, "you look older, Joe."

"I *am* older."

About twelve miles farther west, Arlene said abruptly, "Hey . . . welcome to the Twenty-first Century."

"It arrived inside, too," said Kurtz.

"How could you tell?"

"Good point," said Kurtz and they were silent for another ten miles or so.

Arlene ran her window down and lit a cigarette, batting the ashes out into the brisk autumn air.

"I thought your husband doesn't like it when you smoke."

"Alan died six years ago."

Kurtz nodded and watched the fields go by.

"I guess I could have come to visit you once or twice in eleven years," said Arlene. "Keep you up to speed on things."

Kurtz turned to look at her. "Why? No percentage in that."

Arlene shrugged. "Obviously, I found your message on the machine. But why you thought I'd pick you up after all these years . . ."

"No problem if you didn't," said Kurtz. "The buses still run between Batavia and Buffalo."

Arlene smoked the rest of her cigarette, then tossed it out the window. "Rachel, Sam's little girl—"

"I know."

"Well, her ex-husband got custody, and he still lives in Lockport. I thought you'd want to—"

"I know where he lives," said Kurtz. "Attica has computers and phone books."

Arlene nodded and concentrated on driving.

"You're working with some legal outfit in Cheektowaga?"

"Yeah. Actually, it's three law offices in what used to be a Kwik-Mart in a shopping center. Two of the

firms are ambulance chasers, and the third one is just
a capper mill."

"Does that make you a full-fledged legal secretary?"

Arlene shrugged again. "Mostly I do word processing, spend a lot of time on the phone tracking down
the claimants, and look up the occasional legal crapola
on the Net. The so-called lawyers are too cheap to buy
any law books or DVDs."

"You enjoy it?" asked Kurtz.

She ignored the question.

"They pay you what?" said Kurtz. "Two thousand
or so a month?"

"More than that," said Arlene.

"Well, I'll add five hundred to whatever they're paying you."

She snorted a laugh. "To do what?"

"Same thing you used to do. Just more of it on computers."

"There some miracle going to happen to get you
your P.I. license back, Joe? You have three thousand
bucks a month set aside to pay me?"

"You don't have to be a licensed P.I. to do investigations. Let me worry about paying you. You know
that if I say I will, I will. You think we can get an
office near the old place on East Chippewa?"

Arlene laughed again. "East Chippewa's gotten all
gentrified. You wouldn't recognize the place. Uptight
little boutiques, delis with outside seating, wine and
cheese shops. Rent has gone ballistic there."

"Jesus," said Kurtz. "Well, office space near the
downtown will do. Hell, a basement would do as long
as it has several phone lines and electricity."

Arlene exited the Thruway, paid the toll, and headed south. "Where do you want to go today?"

"A Motel 6 or someplace cheap in Cheektowaga would work."

"Why Cheektowaga?"

"I'm going to have to borrow your car tomorrow morning, and I thought it might be more convenient for you to pick me up on the way to your job. You can give them notice tomorrow morning and pack your stuff, I'll pick you up in the early afternoon, and we can look for the new office."

Arlene lit another cigarette. "You're so considerate, Joe."

Kurtz nodded.

CHAPTER 3

Orchard Park was an upscale area out near the Bills'
Stadium. Arlene's car—although just a basic Buick—
had one of those GPS navigational LCD-screen doo-
hickies set in the dash, but Kurtz never turned it on.
He had memorized the route and had an old road map
if he needed it. He wondered just what in the hell had
happened to people's sense of direction in the last decade if they needed all this electronic shit just to find
their way around.

Most of the homes in Orchard Park were upper-
middle-class or better, but a few were real mansions,
set behind stone walls and iron gates. Kurtz turned into
one of these, gave his name to a speaker grille, and
was told to wait. A video camera mounted on a pillar
by the gate had ceased its slow arcs and now stared
down at him. Kurtz ignored it.

The gate opened and three bodybuilder types in blue blazers and gray slacks came out.

"You can leave the car here," said the smoothest-looking of the three. He gestured for Kurtz to get out of the car.

They frisked him well—even checking his groin area carefully—and then had him unbutton his shirt so that they could see that he wasn't wearing a wire. Then they gestured him onto the back bench of a golf cart and drove him up the long, curving driveway to the house.

Kurtz did not pay much attention to the house. It was your basic brick mansion, a little heavier on security than usual. There was a four-car garage set back to one side, but a Jaguar, a Mercedes, a Honda S2000, and a Cadillac were lined up along the drive. The blue-blazered driver stopped the cart, and the other two men led Kurtz around back to the pool area.

Even though it was October, the pool was still filled and free of leaves. An older man in a paisley robe sat at a poolside table along with a balding middle-aged man in a gray suit. They were drinking coffee from fragile china cups. The bald man refilled the cups from a silver pot as Kurtz and his minders walked up. A fourth bodyguard, this one wearing tight slacks and a polo shirt under his blue blazer, stood with his hands folded over his crotch a few paces behind the old man.

"Sit down, Mr. Kurtz," said the old man. "You'll forgive me if I don't get up. An old injury."

Kurtz sat.

"Coffee?" said the old man.

"Sure."

The bald man poured, but it was obvious that he was no lackey. An expensive metal briefcase lay on the table near him.

"I am Byron Tatrick Farino," said the old man.

"I know who you are," said Kurtz.

The old man smiled slightly. "Do you have a first name, Mr. Kurtz?"

"Are we going to be on a first-name basis, Byron?" The smile faded.

"Watch your mouth, Kurtz," said the bald man.

"Shut up, *consigliere*." Kurtz's eyes never left the old man. "This meeting's between Mr. Farino and me."

"Quite right," said Farino. "But you understand that the meeting is a courtesy and that it would not be taking place at all if you had not . . . ah . . . provided a service to us with regard to my son."

"By keeping Little Skag from being raped up the ass in the showers by Ali and his gang," said Kurtz. "Yeah. You're welcome. But this meeting is business."

"You want compensation for helping young Stephen?" said the lawyer. He clicked open the briefcase.

Kurtz shook his head. He was still looking at Farino. "Maybe Skag told you what I had to offer."

Farino sipped his coffee. The old man's hands were almost as translucent as the expensive china. "Yes, Stephen sent word via his lawyer that you wanted to offer your services. But what services can you possibly provide us that we do not already have, Mr. Kurtz?"

"Investigations."

Farino nodded but the lawyer showed an unpleasant smile. "You were a private investigator once, Kurtz, but you'll never have a license again. You're on parole, for chrissakes. Why on earth would you think that we need a killer ex-con washed-up P.I. on our payroll?"

Kurtz turned his gaze on the lawyer. "You're Miles," he said. "Skag talked about you. He said you like young boys and that the older and limper you get, the younger they get."

The lawyer blinked. His left cheek blazed with blood, as if Kurtz had slapped him. "Carl," he said. The goon in the straining polo shirt opened his hands and took a step forward.

"If you want Carl around, you'd better jerk his leash," said Kurtz.

Mr. Farino held up one hand. Carl stopped. Farino put his other veined hand on the lawyer's forearm. "Leonard," he said. "Patience. Why do you provoke us, Mr. Kurtz?"

Kurtz shrugged. "I haven't had my morning coffee yet." He drank some.

"We *are* willing to reimburse you for your help with Stephen," said Farino. "Please accept it as a . . ."

"I don't want to be paid for that," said Kurtz. "But I'm willing to help you with your real problem."

"What problem?" said Attorney Miles.

Kurtz looked at him again. "Your accountant, a guy named Buell Richardson, is missing. That's not good news at the best of times for a family like yours; but since Mr. Farino's been forced out . . . retired . . . you don't know what the fuck is going on. The FBI could have turned Richardson and have him stashed in a safe house somewhere, singing his guts out. Or the Gonzagas, the other Western New York family, could have whacked him. Or maybe Richardson is going freelance and will be sending you a note and demands any day now. It might be nice to know ahead of time."

"What makes you think—" Miles began.

"Plus, the only part of the action they left you was the contraband being brought in from La Guardia, up from Florida, and down from Canada," Kurtz said to Farino. "And even before Richardson disappeared, someone had been knocking over your trucks."

"What makes you think that we can't deal with this?" Miles's voice was strained, but under control.

Kurtz turned his gaze back on the old man. "You used to," he said. "But who do you trust now?"

Farino's hand was shaking as he set his cup down in its saucer. "What is your proposal, Mr. Kurtz?"

"I investigate for you. I find Richardson. I bring him back to you if possible. I find out if the truck hijacking is linked with his disappearance."

"And your fees?" said Farino.

"Four hundred dollars a day plus my expenses."

Attorney Miles made a rude sound.

"I don't have too many expenses," continued Kurtz. "A thousand up front for a stake. A bonus if I drag your CPA back in good time."

"How large a bonus?" said Farino.

Kurtz drank the last of the coffee. It was black and rich. He stood up. "I'll leave that to you, Mr. Farino. Now I've got to get going. What do you say?"

Farino rubbed his liver-colored lower lip. "Write the check, Leonard."

"Sir, I don't think—"

"Write the check, Leonard. A thousand dollars advance, you said, Mr. Kurtz?"

"In cash."

Miles counted out the money, all in crisp fifties, and put it in a white envelope.

"You realize, Mr. Kurtz," said the old man, his voice suddenly flat and cold, "that the penalties for failure in situations such as this are rarely restricted to simple loss of payment."

Kurtz nodded.

The old man took a pen from the lawyer's briefcase and jotted on a blank business card. "Contact these numbers if you have information or questions," said Farino. "You are never to come back to this house. You are never again to call me or contact me directly in any way."

Kurtz took the card.

"David, Charles, and Carl will run you down the drive to your car," said Farino.

Kurtz looked Carl in the eye and smiled for the first time that morning. "Your bitches can follow me if they want," he said. "But I'll walk. And they'll stay at least ten paces behind me."

CHAPTER 4

There was a Ted's in Orchard Park now and another one in Cheektowaga, but Kurtz drove downtown to the old Ted's Hot Dogs on Porter, near the Peace Bridge. He ordered three of the Jumbos with everything on them, including hot sauce, an order of onion rings, and coffee, and took the cardboard carton to a picnic table near the fence overlooking the river. A few families, some business types and a couple of street people were also having lunch. Leaves fell silently from the big old maple tree. The traffic on the Peace Bridge hummed softly.

There hadn't been many things that you couldn't get in Attica. A Ted's Hot Dog had been one of them. Kurtz remembered Buffalo winter nights in the years before the Ted's on Sheridan had put on its inside dining room: midnight, ten below, three feet of snow, and thirty people lined up outside for dogs.

Finished, he drove north on the Scajaquada Expressway to the Youngman, east to Millersport Highway, and then northeast the fifteen miles or so to Lockport. It did not take him long to find the little house on Lilly Street. Kurtz parked across the street for a few minutes. The house was fairly common for Lockport: a basic white-brick house in a nice old neighborhood. Trees overarched the street; yellow leaves fell. Kurtz looked at the dormer windows on the second floor and wondered which one was her room.

He drove to the nearest middle school. He did not park there, but drove by slowly. Cops were edgy around public schools and wouldn't be especially generous with a recently paroled killer who hadn't even checked in with his P.O. yet.

It was just a building. Kurtz didn't know what he had expected. Middle-school kids didn't go outside for recess. He glanced at his watch and drove back to town, taking the 990 back to save some time.

Arlene led the way into the X-rated video store. The place was half a block from the bus station. Glass from countless broken crack bottles crunched underfoot. A used hypodermic syringe lay in the corner of the doorway vestibule. Most of the storefront window had been painted over, but the unpainted part above eye level was so filthy that no one could have seen into the store even if there had been no paint.

Inside it was every X-rated video store Kurtz had ever seen: a bored, acne-scarred man reading a racing form behind the counter, three or four furtive men pouring over the magazines and videos on the shelves, one junkie female in black leather eyeing the customers, and an assortment of dildos, vibrators, and other sex toys in the glass display case. The only difference was that a lot of the videos were now on DVD.

"Hey, Tommy," Arlene said to the man behind the counter.

"Hey, Arlene," said Tommy.

Kurtz looked around. "Nice," he said. "We doing our Christmas shopping early?"

Arlene led the way down a narrow hall past the peep-show booths, past a toilet with a hand-lettered sign reading DON'T EVEN THINK ABOUT DOING IT IN HERE, ASSHOLES, through a bead curtain, through an unmarked door, and down a steep flight of stairs.

The basement was long and musty and smelled of rat droppings, but the place had been partitioned into two areas with a low railing separating them. Empty bookcases still lined three of the walls. There were long, nicked tables in the outer area and a metal desk in the far space.

"Exits?" said Kurtz.

"That's the good part," said Arlene.

She showed him a rear entrance, separate from the video store, steep stone steps, a steel-reinforced door opening onto the alley. Back in the basement, she went over and swung a bookcase out, revealing another door. She took a key out of her purse and unlocked the padlock on the door. It opened onto an empty underground parking garage.

"When this place was a real bookstore, they sold heroin out of the sci-fi section down here. They liked to have several exits."

Kurtz looked around and nodded. "Phone lines?"

"Five of them. I guess they had a lot of queries about their sci-fi."

"We won't need five," said Kurtz. "But three would be nice." He checked the electrical outlets in the floor and walls. "Yeah, tell Tommy this will do nicely."

"No view."

"That doesn't matter," said Kurtz.

"Not to you," said Arlene. "You won't be here much if it's like the old days. But I'll be looking at these basement walls nine hours a day. I won't even know what season it is."

"This is Buffalo," said Kurtz. "Assume it's winter."

He drove her to her townhouse and helped carry in the cardboard boxes with all of her personal stuff from the Kwik-Mart law offices. There wasn't much. A framed photo of her and Alan. Another photo of their dead son. A hairbrush and some other junk.

"Tomorrow we lease the computers and buy some phones," said Kurtz.

"Oh? With what money?"

Kurtz removed the white envelope from his jacket pocket and gave her $300 in fifties.

"Wow," said Arlene. "That'll buy the handset part of the phone. Maybe."

"You must have some money saved up," said Kurtz.

"You making me a partner?"

"No," said Kurtz. "But I'll pay the usual vig on the loan."

Arlene sighed and nodded.

"And I need to use your car tonight."

Arlene got a beer out of the refrigerator. She did not offer him one. She poured some beer into a clean glass and lit a cigarette. "Joe, you know what all this car borrowing is going to do to my social life?"

"No," said Kurtz, pausing by the door. "What?"

"Not one damned thing."

CHAPTER 5

As lawyer Leonard Miles watched the millions of tons of water flowing hypnotically over the blue-green edge of infinity, he thought of what Oscar Wilde had said about Niagara Falls: "For most people, it's the second biggest disappointment of their honeymoon." Or something like that. Miles was no expert on Wilde.

Miles was watching the falls from the American side—decidedly inferior viewing to the Canadian side—but necessary, since the two men Miles was meeting here probably could not cross into Canada legally. As with most native Buffalonians, Miles rarely paid attention to Niagara Falls, but this was the kind of public place where a lawyer might run into one of his clients—Malcolm Kibunte had been his client—and it was not too far from Miles's home on Grand Island. And Miles had little worry about running into any of the Farinto Family or, more important to Miles, into any of his professional or social peers at the Falls on a workday afternoon.

"Thinking about jumping, Counselor?" came a deep voice from behind him as a heavy hand fell on his shoulder.

Miles started. He turned slowly to look at the grinning face and gleaming diamond tooth of Malcolm Kibunte. Malcolm still had a firm grip on Miles's shoulder, as if considering whether or not to lift the lawyer and throw him over the railing.

He would have, too, Miles knew. Malcolm Kibunte gave him the creeps, and his buddy Cutter actively scared him. Since Leonard Miles had spent much of the last three decades of his life around made men, professional killers, and psychotic drug dealers, he paid some attention to these anxieties. Looking at them both now, Miles did not know which man was stranger looking—Malcolm, the athletic six-foot-three black man with his shaved head, wrestler's body, eight gold rings, six diamond earrings, one diamond-studded front tooth, and ubiquitous black leather outfit, or Cutter, the silent, anorectic-looking near-albino, with his junkie eyes looking like holes melted through white plastic and long, greasy hair hanging down over his grubby sweatshirt.

"What the fuck you want, Miles, calling our asses all the way out here to this fucking place?" said Malcolm, releasing the lawyer.

Miles grinned affably, thinking, *Jesus Christ, I defend the scum of the earth.* In truth, he had never really represented Cutter. He had no idea if Cutter had ever been arrested. He had no idea what Cutter's real name was. Malcolm Kibunte was obviously an acquired name, but Miles had represented the big man—successfully, thank God—in two murder raps (one involving Malcolm's strangling of his wife), a cop shooting, a drug-ring bust, a statutory-rape case, a regular rape case, four aggravated-assault cases, two grand-larceny trials, and some parking violations. The lawyer knew that this did not make them good buddies. In fact, he thought again that Malcolm was precisely the type who would have tossed him over the falls on a whim if it weren't for two factors: (1) Miles worked for the Farino Family, and although the family was a pale shadow of its former self, they still commanded some respect on the street, and (2) Malcolm Kibunte knew that he would need Miles's legal skills again.

Miles led the way apart from the other tourists, motioned the other two to a park bench. Miles and Malcolm sat. Cutter remained standing, staring at nothing. Miles clicked open his briefcase and handed Malcolm a file folder.

Malcolm opened the folder and looked at the mug shots clipped to the top sheet.

"Recognize him?" said Miles.

"Uh-uh," said Malcolm. "But the fucking name sounds sort of familiar."

"Cutter?" said Miles.

"Cutter don't recognize him neither," said Malcolm. Cutter had not even looked in the general direction of the photographs. He hadn't yet looked at Miles. He wasn't even looking at the roaring falls. "You bring us out here so early in the fucking day to look at a picture of some motherfucking honky?" said Malcolm.

"He just got out of—"

"Kurtz," interrupted Malcolm. "That German for 'short,' Miles, my man. This fucker short?"

"Not especially," said Miles. "How'd you know that 'kurtz' was German for 'short'?"

Malcolm gave him a look that would have made a lesser man wet his pants. "I drive me a fucking Mercedes SLK, man. That's what the fucking 'K' in fucking 'SLK' stand for, asshole . . . 'short.' You think I'm a fucking illiterate, you bald college-boy asshole guinea-ass-licking piece-a-shit mouthpiece?" All of this was said without heat or emphasis.

"No, no," said Miles, waving his hands in the air as if shooing away insects. He glanced at Cutter. Cutter did not appear to be listening. "No, I was just impressed," Miles said to Malcolm. "SLK is a great car. Wish I had one."

"No wonder," Malcolm said conversationally. "Drivin' around that fucking piece of American pig-iron Cadillac shit you got."

Miles nodded and shrugged at the same time. "Yes, well, anyway, this Kurtz showed up at Mr. Farino's place with an introduction from Little Skag—"

"Yeah, that's where I hear the fucking name," said Malcolm. "Attica. Motherfucker named Kurtz wasted Ali, leader of the Death Mosque brothers up in Cellblock D, 'bout a year ago. Mosque brothers put ten thousand out for whoever kill the white motherfucker, every nigger motherfucker in Attica sharpening shanks out of fucking spoons and angle irons. Even some of the fucking guards hot for the payoff, but somehow nobody get to this Kurtz motherfucker. If that the same Kurtz. You think it the same, Cutter?"

Cutter turned his grub white face in Malcolm's general direction, but said nothing. Miles looked at Cutter's pale gray eyes in that dead face and shuddered.

"Yeah, I think so, too," said Malcolm. "Why you showin' us this shit, Miles?"

"Kurtz is going to work for Mr. Farino."

"Mr. Farino," parroted Malcolm in a mincing falsetto. He flashed his diamond tooth at Cutter as if he had made a profound witticism. Malcolm's laugh was deep, low, and unnerving. *"Mr. Farino* be a dried-up piece of wop shit with shriveled-up balls. Don't deserve no 'Mister' no more, Miles, my man."

"Be that as it may," said Miles, "this Kurtz—"

"Tell me where Kurtz lives, and Cutter and me will collect the Death Mosque ten thousand."

The lawyer shook his head. "I don't know where he lives. He's only been out of Attica for about forty-eight hours. But he wants to investigate some things for Mr. . . . for the Farino family."

" 'Vestigate?" said Malcolm. "What the fucker think he is, Sherlock Motherfucking Holmes?"

"He used to be a private investigator," said Miles, nodding toward the folder as if urging Malcolm to read the few pages in it. When Malcolm didn't, Miles went on, "Anyway, he's looking into Buell Richardson's disappearance and also into some of the truck hijackings."

Malcolm flashed his diamond tooth again. "Whoa! Now I see why you want us way up here in Honky Tourist World so early in the day. Miles, my man, you must've shit your three-pleats when you heard that."

This was the second time that Malcolm had mentioned how early in the day it was, Miles noted. He did not point out that it was after 3:00 P.M. He said, "We don't want this Kurtz to be messing with these things, do we, Malcolm?"

Malcolm Kibunte pursed his lips in mock solemnity and slowly shook his gleaming, hairless head. "Aww, no, Miles, my man. *We* don't want nobody messing around in what *we* could get our fucking lawyer head blown off for, do *we, Counselor?"*

"No," Cutter added in a voice lacking all human tone, *"we* don't, do *we?"*

Miles literally jumped at the sound of Cutter's voice. He turned and looked at Cutter, who was still staring at nothing. It was as if the words had come from his belly or chest.

"How much?" said Malcolm, no longer playful.

"Ten thousand," said Miles.

"Fuck that. Even with the Death Mosque ten, that ain't enough."

Miles shook his head. "This can't get out. No word to the Mosque brothers. We have to make Kurtz disappear."

"Dis-ap-pear," said Malcolm, stretching out the syllables. "Disappearing some motherfucker harder than just capping him. We talking fifty bills."

Miles showed his most disdainful lawyer smile. "Mr. Farino could call in his best professional talent for less than that."

"Mr. Farino," minced Malcolm, "ain't calling in nobody for nothing, is he, Miles, my man? This Kurtz

your problem—am I right or am I right?"

Miles made a gesture.

"And besides, *Mr. Farino's best professional talent* can kiss my serene black ass and eat wop shit and die wop slow, they get in my way," Malcolm continued.

Miles said nothing.

"What Cutter wants to know," said Malcolm, "is do you or don't you have *nothing* on Kurtz? Not where he live? Not where he work? Friends? Nothing . . . am I right or am I right? Me and Cutter supposed to play P.I. as well as cap this fucker for you?"

"The folder"—began Miles, nodding toward it—"has some information. Where Kurtz used to have an office on Chippewa. The name of a former associate, dead, a woman . . . the name and current address of his former secretary and a few other people he spent time with. Mr. Fi . . . the family had me check on him when Little Skag sent word that Kurtz wanted a meeting. There's not much there, but it could help."

"Forty," said Malcolm. It was not a proposal, merely a final statement. "That only twenty each for C and me. And it's *hard* to disappoint the Mosque that way, Miles, my man."

"All right," said the lawyer. "A fourth up front. As usual." He looked around, saw only tourists, and handed across his second envelope of cash in two days.

Malcolm smiled broadly and counted the $10,000, showing it to Cutter, who seemed to be absorbed in looking at a squirrel near the trash bin.

"You want pictures, as always?" said Malcolm as he slid the envelope into his black leather jacket.

Miles nodded.

"What you do with those Polaroids, Miles, my man? Jack off to them?"

Miles ignored that. "You sure you can do this, Malcolm?"

For a second, Miles thought that he had gone too far. Various emotions rippled across Malcolm's face, like wind rippling an ebony flag, but the final reaction seemed to be humor.

"Oh, yesss," said Malcolm, looking up at Cutter to share his good humor. "Mistah Kurtz, he *dead*."

CHAPTER 6

South Buffalo's Lackawanna had gone belly up as a steel town years before Kurtz had been sent away, but driving south on the elevated expressway now made him think of some sci-fi movie about a dead industrial planet. Below the expressway stretched mile after mile of dark and empty steel mills, factories, black brick warehouses, parking lots, train tracks, rusting rolling stock, smokeless chimneys, and abandoned worker housing. At least Kurtz hoped that those shitty tarpaper shacks on darkened streets under shot-out streetlights were abandoned.

He exited, drove several blocks past hovels and high-fenced yards, and pulled into one of the darkened mills. The gate padlock was unlocked. He drove through, closed the huge gate behind him, and drove to the far end of a parking lot that had been built to

hold six or seven thousand cars. There was one vehicle
there now: a rusted-out old Ford pickup with a camper
shell on the back. Kurtz parked Arlene's Buick next to
it and made the long, dark walk into the main factory
building.

The main doors were open wide. Kurtz's footfalls
echoed in the huge space as he passed slag heaps, cold
open hearths, hanging crucibles the size of houses,
gantries and cranes stripped of everything worth anything, and many huge, rusted shapes he couldn't begin
to identify. The only lighting was from the occasional
yellow trouble light.

Kurtz stopped beneath what had once been a control
room thirty feet above the factory floor. A dim light
illuminated the dirty glass on three sides of the box.
An old man came out onto the metal balcony and
shouted down, "Come on up."

Kurtz climbed the steel ladder.

"Hey, Doc," said Kurtz as the two men walked into
the soft light of the control room.

"Howdy, Kurtz," said Doc. The old man had disappeared into that never-never land of indeterminate
age that some men occupy for decades—somewhere
over sixty-five but definitely under eighty-five.

"It seemed weird to see your pawnshop turned into
an ice-cream parlor," said Kurtz. "I never thought
you'd sell the shop."

Doc nodded. "Fucking economy just stayed too
good in the nineties. I like the watchman job better.
Don't have to worry about doped-up shitheads trying
to knock me over. What can I do you for, Kurtz?"

Kurtz liked this about Doc. It had been more than eleven years since he had seen the old man, but Doc had just used up his entire inventory of small talk.

"Two pieces," said Kurtz. "One semiauto and the other a concealed-carry revolver."

"Cold?"

"As cold as you can make them."

"That's *very* cold." Doc went into the padlocked back room. He came back out in a minute and set several metal cases and small boxes on his cluttered desk. "I remember that nine-millimeter Beretta you used to love so much. What ever happened to that weapon?"

"I buried it with honors," Kurtz said truthfully. "What do you have for me?"

"Well, look at this first," said Doc and opened one of the gray carrying cases. He lifted out a black semiautomatic pistol. "Heckler & Koch USP .45 Tactical," he said. "New. Beautiful piece. Grooved dust cover for lasers or lights. Threaded extended barrel for silencer or suppressor."

Kurtz shook his head. "I don't like plastic guns."

"Polymer," corrected Doc.

"*Plastic.* You and I are made mostly of polymers, Doc. The gun is plastic and glass fiber. It looks like something Luke Skywalker would use."

Doc shrugged.

"Besides," said Kurtz, "I don't use lasers, lights, silencers, or suppressors, and I don't like German guns."

Doc put away the H&K. He opened another case.

"Nice," said Kurtz, lifting out the semiautomatic pistol. It was dark gray—almost black—and constructed primarily of forged steel.

"Kimber Custom .45 ACP," said Doc. "Owned briefly by a little old lady from Tonawanda who just hauled it down to the firing range once or twice a month."

Kurtz racked the slide, checked that the chamber was empty, dropped out the seven-round magazine, made sure that it was empty, slapped the magazine back in, and sighted down the barrel. "Good balance," he said. "But it has a full-length spring guide rod."

"Best kind," said Doc.

"Raises the risk of a loading malfunction," said Kurtz.

"Not on the Kimber. Like I said, custom-made."

"I've never owned a custom weapon," said Kurtz, putting the 1911-style pistol in his waistband and drawing it a few times.

"McCormick low-profile combat sights," said Doc.

"Catches cloth or leather," said Kurtz. "They should use ramp sights on all these fighting guns."

Doc shrugged. "You won't find many of those."

"I prefer double-actions."

"Yeah," said Doc. "I remember that you used to carry cocked and locked. But the Kimber has a sweet trigger pull."

Kurtz dry-fired the weapon several times and nodded. "How much?"

"It cost $675 new just a couple of years ago."

"That's what the little old lady from Tonawanda would've paid," said Kurtz. "How much?"

"Four hundred."

Kurtz nodded. "I'll need to fire some rounds."

"That's what the slag heap down there is for," said Doc. "I got some paper targets in back. I'll throw in a few boxes of Black Hills 185-grain."

Kurtz shook his head. "I'll be using 230-grain."

"Got those, too," said Doc.

"I'll need some leather."

"I got a CYA small-of-the-back. Used, but just nicely broken in. Clean. Twenty bucks."

"Okay," said Kurtz.

"Good. So you've got your home-defense weapon. What do you want to see in the concealed-carry revolver line? Interested in an AirLite Ti?"

"Titanium?" said Kurtz. "Hell, no. I didn't get so old and weak on vacation that I can't lift a pound or two of blue steel."

"Don't look like you did," Doc said and opened a cardboard box. "Can't get much more basic than this, Kurtz. S&W Model 36 Special."

Kurtz checked the heft, inspected the five empty chambers, held the barrel to the light, flipped shut the cylinder and dry-fired it. "How much?"

"Two hundred and fifty."

"Throw the semiauto holster in that."

Doc nodded.

"If I can put five into a three-inch circle at fifty feet with this, it's a deal," said Kurtz.

"Going deer hunting?" Doc said dryly. "You'll need a sandbag rest at that distance. Barrel under two inches, generally the best plan is to sneak up on the deer and shove the Special against its belly before pulling the trigger."

"I noticed a few sandbags down there."

"Speaking of deer hunting," said Doc. "You hear that Manny Levine is looking for you?"

"Who's Manny Levine?"

"A psycho. Brother of Sammy Levine."

"Who's Sammy Levine?"

"Was," said Doc. "Sammy disappeared about eleven-and-a-half years ago. Word on the street was that you helped him get started in the energy business."

"Energy business?"

"Methane production," said Doc.

"Don't know either of them," said Kurtz. "But in case this Manny comes calling, what does he look like?"

"Sort of like Danny DeVito on a bad day. But a much shittier disposition. Carries a .44 Magnum Ruger Redhawk and likes to use it."

"That's a lot of gun for a short fat man," said Kurtz. "Thanks for the heads-up."

Doc shrugged again. "Need anything else tonight?"

"Sap," said Kurtz.

"Regular, ballistic cloth, or leather?"

It was after midnight when Kurtz drove back to Cheektowaga with the .45 holstered in the small of his back, the .38 in his left jacket pocket, and the two-pound sap in his right jacket pocket. He stayed at or under the speed limit all the way back. It would be embarrassing to be stopped by a cop and his license was eight years out of date.

He had just pulled into the Motel 6 when he noticed the sports car parked far from the light, its cloth top up. A red Honda S2000. It could be coincidence, except Kurtz did not believe in coincidence. He made a quick U-turn and drove back out onto the boulevard.

The S2000 switched on its lights and accelerated hard to follow.

CHAPTER 7

Kurtz drove about three miles before deciding that whoever was behind the wheel of the Honda was a fucking idiot. The driver hung so far back that several times Kurtz had to slow down after stoplights or turns to let him catch up.

Kurtz drove away from the lights, down a county road he remembered from the old days. The urban sprawl hadn't stretched this far and the road was empty of traffic. Kurtz accelerated until the sports car had to rush to keep up and was only forty or fifty feet behind him, and then he swerved off on a paved turnout, braking hard, swinging the protesting Buick into a clean 180-degree skidding turn. His headlights illuminated the S2000 as it came to a stop twenty feet away. Only the driver's head was visible.

Kurtz scrambled out, crouched behind the driver's-side door of the Buick, and pulled out the .45 Kimber.

A huge man stepped out of the sports car. His hands were empty.

"Kurtz, you asshole. Come out of there, goddamn you."

Kurtz sighed, slid the .45 into its holster, and stepped out into the headlights' glare. "You don't want to do this, Carl."

"The fuck I don't," said the big Farino-family body-guard.

"Who sent you?"

"Nobody sent me, asshole."

"Then you're dumber than you look," said Kurtz. "If that's possible."

Carl stepped closer. He was wearing the same tight pants and polo shirt as before, without the blazer, showing his pecs despite the chilly night air. "I'm not packing heat, cocksucker," he said.

"Okay," said Kurtz.

"Let's settle this—" said the bodybuilder.

"Settle what?"

"—man to man," said Carl, finishing his thought.

"We're one man short," said Kurtz. He glanced at his watch. The road remained empty.

"Huh?" Carl frowned.

"One thing before going *mano a mano,*" said Kurtz. "How'd you find me?"

"Followed you when you left Mr. Farino's."

Christ, I'm slipping! thought Kurtz with the first alarm he had felt since identifying the hulking body-guard in the sports car.

Carl took another step closer. "No one calls me a bitch," he said, extending the muscles in his powerful forearms and flexing his huge hands.

"Really?" said Kurtz. "I thought you'd be used to it."

Carl lunged.

Kurtz sidestepped him and sapped him over his left ear. Carl went face first onto the Buick bumper and then again onto the asphalt. Kurtz heard teeth snapping off on both impacts. Kurtz walked over and kicked him in the ass. Carl did not stir.

Kurtz went back to the Buick to switch off its lights, then did the same with the sports car, shutting off its engine, locking the doors, and tossing the keys into the woods. Grunting slightly, he dragged Carl around to the left rear of the Buick and kicked his legs into line just in front of the left rear wheel.

Then Kurtz got back in Arlene's car, made sure no one was coming, tuned the radio to an all-night blues station, and drove away, switching on the lights once he was on the highway, heading back to the Motel 6 to check out.

CHAPTER 8

"Of all the unbelievable nerve," said Attorney Leonard Miles. "Of all the unmitigated gall."

"Incredible balls, you mean," said Don Farino.

"Whatever," said Miles.

There were three of them in the huge solarium, not counting the mynah bird who was carrying on his own raucous conversation in his cage amidst the riot of green plants. Farino was in his wheelchair, but as was his custom when in the wheelchair, he was dressed in a suit and tie. His twenty-eight-year-old daughter Sophia sat on the green, silk-upholstered settee under the palm fronds. Miles was pacing back and forth.

"Which part do you think took the nerve," asked Sophia, "crippling Carl or calling us last night to tell us about it?"

"Both," said Miles. He stopped pacing and crossed his arms. "But especially the call. Absolute arrogance."

"I heard the tape of the call," said Sophia. "He didn't sound arrogant. He sounded like someone phoning to let you know that your dry cleaning is ready for pickup."

Miles glanced at Farino's daughter but looked at her father when he spoke next. He hated dealing with the woman. Farino's oldest son, David, had been capable enough, but had wrapped his Dodge Viper around a telephone pole at 145 miles per hour. The second son, Little Skag, was hopeless. The Don's older daughter, Angelina, had run away to Europe years before. That left this . . . girl.

"Either way, sir," Miles said to the former don, "I think that we should call in the Dane."

"Really?" said Byron Farino. "You think it's that serious, Leonard?"

"Yes, sir. He crippled one of your people and then called to brag about it."

"Or perhaps he just called to save us the embarrassment of finding out about Carl's injuries in the newspaper," said Sophia. "This way we were able to get out to the accident scene first."

"*Accident* scene," repeated Miles, not hiding his derision.

Sophia shrugged. "Our people made it look like an accident. It saved us a lot of questions and legal expenses."

Miles shook his head. "Carl was a brave and loyal employee."

"Carl was an absolute idiot," said Sophia Farino. "All those steroids obviously burned out what little brain he had left."

Miles turned to say something sharp to the bitch and instantly thought better of it. He stood in silence, listening to the mynah bird berate an invisible opponent.

"Leonard," said Don Farino, "what was the first thing Carl said to our people when he regained consciousness this morning?"

"He couldn't say anything. His jaw is wired shut, and he'll need extensive oral surgery before—"

"What did he *write* to Buddy and Frank, then?" asked Don Farino.

The attorney hesitated. "He wrote that five of Gonzaga's people followed him and jumped him," Miles said after a moment.

Don Farino nodded slowly. "And if we had believed Carl . . . if Kurtz had not called last night . . . if I had not called Thomas Gonzaga this morning, we could be at war, could we not, Leonard?"

Miles showed his hands and shrugged. "Carl was embarrassed. He was in pain—medicated—and afraid we'd blame him."

"He followed this Kurtz and tried to settle his private scores on family time," said Sophia Farino. "Then he screwed *that* up. Why shouldn't we blame him?"

Miles only shook his head and gave Don Farino a look that said, *Women can't understand these things.*

Byron Farino shifted slightly in his wheelchair. It was obvious that he was in pain from the eight-year-old gunshot wound and the bullet still embedded near his spine. "Write a check for $5,000 for Carl's family," said the Don. "Is it just his mother?"

"Yes, sir," said Miles, not seeing any reason to mention that Carl lived with a twenty-year-old male model of Miles's acquaintance.

"Would you see to that, Leonard?" said Farino.

"Of course." Miles hesitated and then decided to be bold. "And the Dane?"

Farino was quiet for a moment. The mynah bird deep in the green fronds chattered away to itself. Finally the older don said, "Yes, I think perhaps a call to the Dane would be in order."

Miles blinked. He was pleasantly surprised. This would save him $30,000 with Malcolm and Cutter. Miles had no intention of demanding the advance money back. "I'll contact the Dane—" he began.

Farino shook his head. "No, no, I'll take care of it, Leonard. You go make out the check for Carl's family and make sure that it's delivered. Oh, and Miles . . . what was the rest of Mr. Kurtz's message last night?"

"Just where we could find Carl. Kurtz had the gall— I mean, he said that it hadn't been personal—and then he said that he wouldn't be starting his $400-a-day retainer until today. That he would be interviewing Buell Richardson's wife this morning."

"Thank you, Leonard." Farino dismissed the lawyer.

When Miles was gone, Farino turned to his daughter. As was true of his older daughter, he saw much of their late mother there: the full lips, the olive complexion, the mass of black hair curling around her oval face, the long, sensuous fingers, and the lush body. But he had to admit that Sophia's eyes showed more intelligence and depth than his wife's ever had.

Farino sat lost in thought for a long minute. The mynah stirred in its cage but respected the silence. Eventually Farino said, "Do you feel comfortable taking care of this, Sophia?"

"Of course, Papa."

"Dealing with the Dane can be . . . disturbing," said her father.

Sophia smiled. "I was the one who wanted to be involved in the family business, Papa," she said. "*All* of the family business."

Farino nodded unhappily. "But with the Dane . . . be very, very careful, my dear. Even on the secure telephone line, be very professional."

"Of course, Papa."

Out on the lawn of the mansion, Leonard Miles had to work to keep from smiling. *The Dane.* But the more he thought about it, the more sense it made that this mess be cleaned up *before* the Dane became involved. And Miles certainly did not want to do anything that would irritate Malcolm and his partner. Even the thought of the Dane, Malcolm, and Cutter crossing paths made Miles a bit dizzy. And although *Mrs.* Richardson knew nothing, Miles realized now that she might be considered a loose end.

You keep tying up all of these loose ends, scolded the parsimonious part of Miles's mind, *and you'll end up in the poorhouse.*

Miles paused to think about that. Finally he shook his head. He was caviling about a few thousand more dollars when millions—*millions*—were involved. He flipped open his phone and called Malcolm Kibunte's number. Malcolm never answered the phone in person.

"Our K package will be arriving at the accountant's wife's home sometime this morning," he said to the answering machine. "It would be a good place to pick up that package." He hesitated only a second. "And *her* package should probably be picked up at the same time. I'll pay for delivery of both items when we meet again. Please bring along the receipts."

Miles flipped the phone shut and walked down to his Cadillac to write the check for Carl's mother. Miles was not worried about using the cell phone because he would throw the phone into the river on the drive back into town. He owned many such phones, none of them traceable to Counselor Leonard Miles.

Driving toward the main gate, he decided that he would break the news to Carl's roommate himself.

CHAPTER 9

It was raining hard when Kurtz walked up to the sprawling brick home just a few blocks from Delaware Park. Malcolm and Cutter watched from Malcolm's yellow SLK, its top up, half a block back from where Kurtz had just parked his Buick. Malcolm had noticed how careful Kurtz had been, driving by once to case the place, checking several times that he had not been followed before parking. But Malcolm and Cutter had arrived first and had hunkered down when Kurtz drove past. The driving rain helped conceal them in the car, but Malcolm had turned the engine off anyway. He knew that nothing gave away the presence of a watcher faster than the exhaust from an idling engine.

Cutter made a soft noise from the passenger seat.

"In a minute, C, my man," said Malcolm. "In a minute."

*   *   *

Kurtz had not known many accountants over the years—he'd had a couple as divorce-case clients and had seen a few more adventurous types serving time in Attica for whatever white-collar crimes accountants commit—but Mrs. Richardson hardly seemed like an accountant's wife to him. She seemed more like one of the expensive call girls who plied their trade near the fancier Niagara Falls resort hotels. Kurtz had seen pictures of Buell Richardson and heard descriptions from Little Skag. The accountant had been short, bald, in his fifties, peering out at the world through thick glasses like a myopic, arrogant chipmunk. His wife was in her late twenties, very blond, very built, and—it seemed to Kurtz—very chipper for a probable widow.

"Please sit down, Mr. Kurtz. Just don't move that chair out of its place, please. The furniture placement is part of the general ambience."

"Sure," said Kurtz, having not the slightest clue as to what she was talking about. Buell Richardson had been rich enough to own a Frank Lloyd Wright home near Delaware Park. "Not *the* Frank Lloyd Wright house near Delaware Park," Arlene had said after making the interview appointment for him. "Not the Dewey D. Martin house. The other one."

"Right," Kurtz had said. Kurtz didn't know the Dewey D. Martin house from a housing project, but he had found the address easily enough. Thought the home was nice enough looking if you liked all that brick and the overhanging eaves, but the straight-backed chairs near the fireplace were a literal pain in the butt. He had no idea if Frank Lloyd Wright had designed the chairs and he certainly did not care, but he *was* certain that the chair had not been built with any regard for the human body. The chair back was as stiff and upright as an ironing board and the seat was too small for a midget's ass. If they had designed an electric chair this way, Kurtz thought, the condemned man would bitch about it in his last seconds before they threw the switch.

"It's nice of you to agree to talk to me, Mrs. Richardson."

"Anything to help in the investigation, Mr. . . . ."

"Kurtz."

"Yes. But you're not with the police, you say. A private investigator?"

"An investigator, yes, ma'am," said Kurtz. When he had been a real P.I., he had owned one good suit and two decent ties for such interviews, and now he felt foolish in his Eddie Bauer windbreaker and chinos. Arlene had given him one of Alan's old ties, but Kurtz was two inches taller and forty pounds heavier than his secretary's dead husband, so there would be no suit from that source. Kurtz looked forward to earning some money. After purchasing the two pistols, giving Arlene $300 toward equipment, and paying for his food and lodging, Kurtz was down to about $35.

"Who else is interested in finding Buell?" asked the accountant's wife.

"I'm not at liberty to reveal my client's identity, ma'am. But I can assure you that it's someone who wishes your husband well and wants to help find him."

Mrs. Richardson nodded. Her hair was tied up in an elaborate bun and Kurtz found himself noticing the artfully loose wisps of blond hair touching her perfect neck. "Is there anything that you might tell me about the circumstances of Mr. Richardson's disappearance?"

She shook her head slowly. "I've reported everything to the police, of course. But there's honestly nothing out of the ordinary that I can recall. It was just a month ago this Thursday. Buell left at his usual time that morning . . . eight-fifteen . . . and said that he was going straight to his office."

"His secretary told us that he didn't have any meetings scheduled for that day," said Kurtz. "Isn't that unusual for an accountant?"

"Not at all," said Mrs. Richardson. "Buell had a very few private clients and much of his business with them was conducted over the telephone."

"You know the names of those clients?"

Mrs. Richardson pursed her perfect pink lips. "I'm sure that's confidential, Mr. . . . ."

"Kurtz."

". . . but I can assure you that all of his clients were important people . . . *serious* people . . . and all above reproach."

"Of course," said Kurtz. "And he was driving the Mercedes E300 on the day of his disappearance?"

Mrs. Richardson cocked her head. "Yes. Haven't you *read* the police report, Mr. . . . ."

"Kurtz. Yes, ma'am, I have. Just double-checking."

"Well, he was. Driving the smaller Mercedes, I mean. I had some shopping to do that day so I had the larger one. The police found the little one the next day. The little Mercedes, I mean."

Kurtz nodded. Little Skag had said that the accountant's E300 had been left in Lackawanna, where it had been stripped within hours. There had been hundreds of fingerprints on the shell of the vehicle, all those identified so far belonging to the gangbangers and civilians who had helped themselves to parts.

"Can you think of any reason for Mr. Richardson to want to drop out of sight?" said Kurtz.

The statuesque blonde snapped her head back as if Kurtz had slapped her. "Do you mean, for instance, another woman, Mr. . . . ."

"Kurtz," said Kurtz and waited.

"I resent that question and its implications."

I don't blame you, Kurtz wanted to say aloud. *If your husband was stalking poon on the side, he was a moron.* He waited.

"No, there was no reason for Buell to want to . . . how did you put it, Mr. Katz? To drop out of sight. He was happy. *We* were happy. We have a good life. Buell was considering retiring in a year or so, we have the place in Maui where we were going to spend time, and we recently bought a boat . . . a little sixty-foot catamaran. . . . " Mrs. Richardson paused. "We planned to spend the next few years sailing around the world."

Kurtz nodded. *'A little sixty-foot catamaran.' What the hell would a* big *boat be like?* He tried to imagine a year on a sixty-foot yacht with this woman, tropical ports, long nights at sea. It wasn't too difficult. "Well, you've been very helpful, Mrs. Richardson," Kurtz said, rose, and headed for the door.

Mrs. Richardson hurried to keep up. "I don't see how my answering these few questions can help find my husband, Mr. . . ."

Kurtz had given up on the name thing. He'd known Sterno sniffers with better short-term memories than this woman.

"Actually, you've been very helpful," he said again. And she had been. Kurtz's only real reason for interviewing her was to see if she might have been involved in the accountant's disappearance. She hadn't been. Mrs. Richardson was beautiful—striking, even—but she obviously wasn't the sharpest knife in the drawer. Her ignorance had not been feigned. Kurtz doubted if she was even aware that her husband was almost certainly decomposing in a shallow grave or being nibbled on by bottom feeders in Lake Erie as they spoke.

"Thanks again," he said and walked out to Arlene's Buick.

"Shit," said Malcolm. He and Cutter were just getting out of the SLK. Malcolm put his hand out as if to grab Cutter, but stopped with his fingers an inch short of the man's arm. He would never touch Cutter without permission, and Cutter would never give such permission. "Wait," said Malcolm, and both men slid back into the car.

Kurtz was coming out of the house. Now that Malcolm could see him more clearly, he realized that Kurtz still looked pretty much like his mug shot: a little older, a little leaner, a little meaner.

"I thought he be in there a while," Malcolm said. "What kind of fucking 'vestigator is he, five minutes with the widow?"

Cutter had taken his gravity knife out of his sweatshirt pocket and now seemed absorbed in the knobby contours of its handle.

"We wait a minute, maybe he'll go back in," said Malcolm.

Kurtz did not go back in. He got in the Buick and drove off.

"Shit," Malcolm said again. Then, "Okay, Miles the mouthpiece say pick up both packages. Which package you think we should pick up first, Cutter, my man?"

Cutter looked at the mansion. His hand twitched and both blades flicked out. The knife was made by a famous riflemaker, and it had two blades. Now Cutter folded one of the blades away and kept the other open and locked. It was a curved blade—razor sharp for four inches, and then sharp but fully hooked at the end. This was known as a gut hook.

Cutter's eyes gleamed.

"Yeah, you right as always," agreed Malcolm. "I know a way we can find Mr. Kurtz again later when we want him. Now we got business here."

The two men got out of the SLK. Malcolm beeped it locked, paused, and then beeped it open again.

"Almost forgot," he said. He pulled out the Polaroid camera and both men walked across the empty street in the rain.

CHAPTER 10

The Erie County Medical Center was a gigantic complex close enough to the Kensington Expressway for the patients to hear the hum of traffic if they wanted. Few did. Most of them were too preoccupied with living and dying and trying to sleep to notice the distant sound of traffic over the whisper of heating or air conditioning, the chimes and announcements, and the chatter in the hallways and rooms. Visiting hours ended officially at 9:00 P.M., but the last of the visitors were usually filtering out around 10:00 P.M.

At 10:15 on this October night, a tall, thin gentleman in a simple tan raincoat and a Bavarian-style hat with a red feather in it stepped off the elevator into the West Wing Intensive Care area. The man was carrying a small bouquet of flowers. He looked to be in his midfifties, with sad eyes, a slightly distracted expression, and a faint smile under a well-groomed ginger mustache. He wore expensive black gloves.

"I'm sorry, sir, visiting hours are over," said the station nurse, intercepting him with her gaze before he took three steps from the elevator.

The tall man paused and looked even more lost. "Yes . . . I am sorry." He had a slight European accent. "I just arrived from Stuttgart. My mother . . ."

"You can visit her in the morning, sir. Visiting hours begin at 10:00 A.M."

The man nodded, began to turn away, then turned back with the flowers extended. "Mrs. Haupt. She is on your chart, yes? I just arrived from Stuttgart, and my brother says that Mumi is in very serious condition."

At the mention of the name, the nurse glanced at her computer screen. Whatever she saw there made her bite her lip. "Mrs. Haupt is your mother, sir?"

"Yes." The tall man in the raincoat shuffled his feet and looked at the flowers. "It has been too many years since I saw her last. I should have come sooner, but work . . . and I must fly home tomorrow."

The station nurse hesitated. Nurses and orderlies were bustling back and forth, bringing the bedtime meds to the patients. "You understand, Mr. . . . Haupt?"

"Yes."

"You understand, Mr. Haupt, that your mother has been in a coma for several weeks now. She won't know you're here."

The sad-eyed man nodded. "But *I* would know that I had been there with her."

The nurse's eyes actually glistened. "Down the hall there, sir. Mrs. Haupt is in one of the private rooms, eleven-oh-eight. I'll have one of the nurses come down and check on you in a few minutes."

"Thank you very much," said the man in the raincoat and shuffled through the whirlwind of purposeful movement and all of its attendant chaos.

Mrs. Haupt was in a coma. Various tubes flowed in and out of her. On the nightstand next to her, her dentures grinned out from a glass of water. The man in the raincoat and the feathered hat took the paper off the stems of the flowers and set them in the glass with the old woman's teeth. Then he glanced out into the corridor, saw no one, and walked quietly down to Room 1123.

There were no guards. Carl was asleep, medicated, when the man entered the room. Carl's head was bandaged, his face was a mass of bruises coalescing into a raccoon mask, and his jaw was wired shut. Both legs were in casts and connected to an elaborate structure of guy wires, counterweights, and a metal frame. Carl's right arm was restrained with a thick strap, and his left arm was taped down to a board so that an IV drip could do its work. He had numerous tubes connected to him.

The tall man quietly unlooped the nurse's call button from the headboard and moved it out of Carl's reach. Then he took a capped syringe from his raincoat pocket and held it in his right hand while he used his other hand to squeeze Carl's heavily wired jaw.

"Carl? Carl?" The man's voice was soft and solic-
itous.

Carl moaned, groaned, tried to turn over, was restrained by all of the straps and wires, and opened his
one good eye. It was obvious that he did not recognize
the man in the raincoat.

The man in the raincoat removed the cover from the
needle with his teeth and drew the plunger back, filling
the empty syringe with air. He softly spat the plastic
cover from his mouth and caught it in the same hand
as the syringe. "Are you awake, Carl?"

Carl's one eye showed groggy confusion fading into
horror as he watched the strange man remove his IV
drip from the monitor, click off the alarm, and slip the
tip of the needle into the drip. Carl tried to roll over
toward the call button. The stranger grasped his IV-
attached arm and held him fast.

"The Farinos wanted to thank you for all of your
faithful service, Carl, and to say that they are sorry
that you were such an idiot." The tall man's voice was
soft. He fitted the syringe needle deeper into the needle
port on the IV-drip attachment. Carl made terrible
noises through his wired-shut jaw and thrashed around
on the bed like some huge fish.

"Shhh," the man said soothingly and pushed the
plunger all the way down. The air bubble was actually
visible in the clear IV tube as it flowed down toward
Carl's forearm.

The tall man expertly recapped the syringe with one
hand and set it back in his raincoat pocket. Holding
Carl's left wrist as he was, studying the watch on his
own right wrist, someone passing by would assume

that this was a doctor on late rounds, taking a patient's pulse.

Carl's broken jaw cracked audibly and wire actually snapped. The sound he made was not quite human.

"Another four or five seconds," the man in the raincoat said softly. "Ahhh, there we are."

The air bubble had hit Carl's heart, essentially exploding it. Carl arched so wildly that two of the metal guy wires strummed like high-tension wires in a high wind. The bodyguard's eyes grew so wide that they seemed ready to burst, but then they glazed over into sightlessness. Blood poured from both of Carl's nostrils.

The man released Carl's wrist, left the room, walked down the short hall in the opposite direction from the nurse's central station, and took the back stairway down to the basement and the ambulance ramp up and out of the hospital.

Sophia Farino was waiting outside in her black Porsche Boxster. The hardtop was up against the rain that continued to fall. The tall man slid into the seat next to her. She did not ask him how things had gone.

"The airport?" she said.

"Yes, please," said the man in the same soft, pleasant tones he had used with Carl.

They drove east on the Kensington for several minutes. "The weather in Buffalo always pleases me," the man said, breaking the silence. "It reminds me of Copenhagen."

Sophia smiled and then said, "Oh, I almost forgot." She unlocked the small center console and brought out a thick white envelope.

The man smiled slightly and put the envelope in his raincoat pocket without counting the money. "Please give my warmest regards to your father," he said.

"I will."

"And if there is any other service I could possibly perform for your family . . ."

Sophia looked away from the tak-tak of the windshield wipers. It was just a few more miles to the airport. "Well, actually," she said, "there is something else. . . ."

CHAPTER 11

Kurtz sat in the tiny Civic Center office, looked across the cluttered desk at his parole officer, and realized that she was cute as a bug.

The P.O.'s name was Peg O'Toole. *P.O. for P.O.*, thought Kurtz. He rarely thought in terms such as "cute as a bug," but that's what Ms. O'Toole was. In her early thirties, probably, but with a fresh, freckled face and clear blue eyes. Red hair—not the astounding, pure red like Sam's, but a complex auburn-red—that fell down to her shoulders in natural waves. A bit overweight by modern standards, which pleased Kurtz to no end. One of the best phrases he had ever encountered was the writer Tom Wolfe's description of New York anorectic socialites as "social X-rays." Kurtz idly wondered what P.O. Peg O'Toole would think of him if he mentioned that he had read Tom Wolfe. Then

Kurtz wondered what was wrong with himself for wondering that.

"So where are you living, Mr. Kurtz?"

"Here and there." Kurtz noticed that she had not condescended to him by calling him by his first name.

"You'll need a fixed address." Her tone was neither familiar nor cold, merely professional. "I have to visit your place of residence in the next month and make sure that it's acceptable under terms of parole."

Kurtz nodded. "I've been staying in a Motel 6, but I'm looking for something more permanent." He didn't think it would be wise to tell her about the abandoned icehouse and the borrowed sleeping bag he currently called home.

Ms. O'Toole made a note. "Have you begun looking for employment yet?"

"Found a job," said Kurtz.

She raised her eyebrows slightly. Kurtz noticed that they were thick and the same color as her hair.

"Self-employed," he said.

"That won't do," said Peg O'Toole. "We'll need to know the details."

Kurtz nodded. "I've set up an investigatory agency."

The P.O. tapped her lower lip with her pen. "You realize, Mr. Kurtz, that you won't be licensed as a private investigator in the state of New York again, and that it's illegal for you to own or carry a firearm or to associate with known felons?"

"Yes," said Kurtz. When the P.O. said nothing, he went on, "It's a legally registered business—'Sweetheart Search.'"

Ms. O'Toole did not quite smile. " 'Sweetheart Search'? Is it some sort of skip-trace service?"

"In a way," said Kurtz. "It's a Web-based locator service. My secretary and I do ninety-nine percent of the work on computers."

The P.O. tapped her white teeth with the capped pen. "There are about a hundred services like that on the Net," she said.

"That's what Arlene, my secretary, said."

"And why do you think yours will make money?"

"First, it's my feeling that there are about a hundred million baby boomers out there approaching retirement who are ready to dump their current spouses and probably still have the hots for old boyfriends or girlfriends from high school," said Kurtz. "You know, memories of first lust in the backseat of the '66 Mustang, that sort of thing."

Ms. O'Toole smiled. "Not much of a backseat in the '66 Mustang," she said. She was not being coy, Kurtz thought, merely observant.

Kurtz nodded. "You like old Mustangs?"

"We're not here to discuss my preference in muscle cars," she said. "Why are these aging baby boomers going to turn to your service? Since there are all these other cheap classmate-tracing sites on the Web?"

"Yes," said Kurtz, "but Arlene and I are being more proactive." He paused. "Did I say 'proactive'? Christ, I hate that word. Arlene and I are being more . . . imaginative."

Ms. O'Toole looked mildly surprised for the second time.

"Anyway, we go through old high-school year-books," said Kurtz, "find someone who might have been popular in his or her class way back when—we're starting in the sixties—and then send the information to former classmates. You know—'Have you ever wondered what happened to Billy Benderbix? Find out through Sweetheart Search'—that sort of garbage."

"You're aware of privacy laws?"

"Yep," said Kurtz. "There aren't enough of them for the Net. But we just look up these former classmates via the usual people finders and send them this bulk E-mail query."

"Is it working?"

Kurtz shrugged. "It's only been a few days, but we've had several hundred hits." He paused. He knew that the P.O. didn't want to make small talk any more than he did; but he wanted to share a story with someone, and there certainly was no one else in his life. "Want to hear about our first try?"

"Sure," said the P.O.

"Well, Arlene has been gathering yearbooks for the past few days. We've accessed back issues from all over the country and ordered more through the mail, but we're starting with the Buffalo area—real year-books—until we get a database started."

"Makes sense."

"So yesterday we're ready to start. I say, 'Let's pick someone at random here to be our first Mr. or Miss Lonely Heart . . . sorry, Ms. Lonely Heart. . . .' "

"That sounds stupid," said O'Toole. "*Miss* Lonely Heart is right."

Kurtz nodded. "So Arlene takes this high-school yearbook from the stack—Kenmore West, 1966—and flips it open. I poke my finger down and choose some-one at random. He had a weird name, but I figure, what the hell. Arlene starts laughing. . . ."

O'Toole's expression was neutral, but she was lis-tening.

"Wolf Blitzer," said Kurtz. " 'I think maybe his classmates will know about him,' says Arlene. 'Why?' I say. So Arlene starts laughing at me. . . ."

"You don't know Wolf Blitzer?" said P.O. O'Toole.

Kurtz shrugged again. "I guess he became well known way back when my trial was going on, and I haven't watched much CNN since."

O'Toole was smiling.

"Anyway," continued Kurtz, "Arlene quits laughing, explains who Wolf Blitzer is and why he wouldn't be our best choice, and then pulls down a West Seneca High School yearbook. Flips it open. Stabs at a picture. Another guy. Tim Russert."

O'Toole laughed softly. "NBC," she said.

"Yeah. I'd never heard of him, either. By this point, Arlene's busting a gut."

"Quite a coincidence."

Kurtz shook his head. "I don't believe in coinci-dence. It was Arlene setting me up. She has a weird sense of humor. Anyway, finally we find someone from a Buffalo-area high school who's *not* a well-known correspondent, and—"

The phone rang. As O'Toole answered it, Kurtz felt some relief at the interruption. He'd been deliberately babbling.

"Yeah . . . yeah . . . okay," O'Toole was saying. "I understand. All right. Good." When she hung up, her gaze seemed cooler to Kurtz.

The door burst open. A homicide cop named Jimmy Hathaway and a younger cop whom Kurtz had never seen before came in with 9mm Glocks aimed, badges visible on their belts. Kurtz looked back to see that Peg O'Toole had pulled a Sig Pro from her purse on the floor and was aiming it at his face.

"Hands behind your head, asshole," shouted Hathaway.

They cuffed Kurtz, frisked him—he was clean, of course, since it hadn't seemed a good idea to pack heat to the first meeting with his P.O.—and then shoved him up against the wall while the younger cop emptied his pockets of change, car keys, and mints.

"You won't be seeing this fucking loser again," Hathaway said to O'Toole as he shoved Kurtz out the door. "He's going back to Attica, and this time he's never coming out."

Kurtz glanced back once at Peg O'Toole before another shove sent him down the hallway. She had set her gun away. Her expression was unreadable.

CHAPTER 12

Kurtz knew that it was not going to be an easy interrogation when Hathaway, the homicide cop, lowered some louvered blinds over the one-way mirror lining one wall of the interrogation room and then ripped the recording-microphone wire out of its jack on the floor. A second bad omen was that Kurtz was handcuffed behind his back to a straight-back metal chair which was, in turn, bolted to the floor. The third clue came from some dark stains on the battered wooden table and more stains spattered on the linoleum floor near the bolted chair, although Kurtz told himself that these could have been from spilled coffee. But perhaps the strongest hint was the fact that Hathaway was pulling on a pair of those latex gloves paramedics use to keep from getting AIDS.

"Welcome back, Kurtz, you fuck," Hathaway said when the blinds were down. He took three quick steps closer and backhanded Kurtz across the face.

Kurtz shook his head and spat blood onto the linoleum. The good news was that Hathaway wasn't wearing the heavy gold ring that he used to wear on his right hand, possibly because it would tear the latex gloves. Kurtz's cheek still bore a faint scar from his ear to the corner of his mouth resulting from a similar chat with Hathaway almost twelve years earlier.

"Nice to see you, too, Lieutenant," said Kurtz.

"It's *Detective*," said Hathaway.

Kurtz shrugged as much as he could while handcuffed. "More than eleven years," he said and spat blood again, "I figured maybe you'd finally been able to pass the lieutenant's exam. Or at least the sergeant's."

Hathaway came forward and hit Kurtz again, this time with his fist closed.

Kurtz faded a bit and came back as the younger cop was saying, ". . . for chrissakes, Jimmy."

"Shut up," said Detective Hathaway. He paced around the table, glancing at his watch. Kurtz guessed that the detective had only so much time for the private part of this interrogation. *That's good,* thought Kurtz, his head still ringing.

"Where were you yesterday morning, Kurtz?" barked Hathaway.

Kurtz shook his head. Mistake. The room pitched and yawed. Only the handcuffs kept him upright in the chair.

"I said, Where *were* you yesterday?" said Hathaway, walking closer.

"Lawyer," said Kurtz. He still had blood in his mouth, but all of his teeth seemed solid.

"What?"

"I want a lawyer."

"Your lawyer's dead, scumbag," said Hathaway. "That ambulance-chasing pimp Murrell had a coronary four years ago."

Kurtz knew that. "Lawyer," he said again.

Hathaway's response was to remove his Glock 9mm from a shoulder holster and a tiny Smith and Wesson .32 from his suit pocket. He tossed the .32 onto the table near Kurtz. A classic plant-it-on-the-perp throwdown.

"Jimmy, for God's sake!" said the younger, shorter cop. Kurtz could not tell if it was part of their choreography or if the younger homicide detective was actually concerned. If it was the standard good-cop, bad-cop farce, then the kid was a pretty good actor.

"Maybe we didn't frisk you well enough coming in," said Hathaway, staring into Kurtz with his pale blue eyes. Kurtz had always thought that Hathaway had flies in his eyes, and a decade later, the cop was crazier than ever.

Hathaway racked a round into the chamber of his Glock. "Where were you yesterday morning, Joey-boy?"

Kurtz was getting bored with this. Over the past decade, he'd had a few conversations with other cons about the Prime Directive of "never kill a cop." Kurtz's point of view, for conversation's sake, had been "Why not?" He had often had Hathaway in mind during these talks.

Kurtz looked away from the red-faced homicide cop and thought about other things.

"You miserable asshole," said Hathaway. He holstered the Glock, disappeared the .32 with a sweep of his hand, and hit Kurtz on the collarbone with a black-jack quite similar to the one that Kurtz had used on Carl. Immediately, Kurtz's entire shoulder and left arm went numb, then raged with pain.

The other detective plugged in the microphone and opened the blinds. Hathaway had peeled off the paramedic gloves. The throwdown and blackjack were out of sight. The Glock was holstered.

Well, thought Kurtz, *that went all right.*

"You acknowledge, Joe Kurtz, that you've been advised of your rights?" said Detective Hathaway.

Kurtz grunted. He didn't think his collarbone was broken, but it would be a few hours before he could use his left arm.

"Where were you yesterday morning between the hours of 9:00 and 11:00 A.M.?" said Hathaway.

"I'd like to speak to an attorney," said Kurtz, enunciating as carefully as he could.

"A public defender is being notified as we speak," Hathaway said to the microphone. "It should be noted that this conversation is being held with the agreement and at the request of Mr. Kurtz."

Kurtz leaned closer to the mike. "Your mother used to suck dick on South Delaware, Detective Hathaway. I was a regular customer."

Hathaway forgot that he was not wearing gloves and backhanded Kurtz so hard that the bloody spray from his nose splattered the wall six feet away. *That was smart of me,* he thought. *They edit these tapes, anyway.* He shook his head. He had flicked his head away from the blow fast enough to avoid a broken nose.

"Do you recognize this woman?" said the other detective, sliding a white folder across the table. He opened the folder.

"Don't drip on the pictures, Kurtz!" warned Hathaway.

Kurtz tried to comply, although there was so much blood visible in the black-and-white photos that a little of the real stuff shouldn't be a problem.

"Do you recognize this woman?" repeated the other detective.

Kurtz said nothing. From the photographs, it was just possible to tell that it had been a woman. Kurtz knew who it was, of course. He recognized the straight-backed chairs around the Frank Lloyd Wright table.

"Do you deny that you were in this woman's home yesterday morning?" demanded the younger detective. And then, to the microphone, he added, "Let the record show that Mr. Kurtz refuses to identify the photograph of Mary Anne Richardson, a woman with whom he met yesterday."

She had a nose, eyes, breasts, and all of her skin yesterday, Kurtz was tempted to say aloud. He did study the photos spread out on the tabletop. The murderer had been an edged-weapons freak, powerful, a full-blown psycho, but good with the blade. For all the slaughterhouse aspect of the vivisection, it had been administered efficiently. Kurtz doubted if Mrs. Richardson would have appreciated that distinction, since it looked as if the cutter had kept her alive for quite a while during the proceedings. Kurtz studied the background, trying to guess the time of the murder from the arrangement of the furniture. The furniture was exactly as he and the lady had left it. There had been no real struggle—or the knife man had been big enough that the struggle had been localized to that small patch of soaked carpet just outside the dining room. Or, most likely, there had been more than one man—one to hold and one to carve.

"Is that semen on her dress?" asked Kurtz.

"Shut up," said Detective Hathaway. He stepped closer, put one hand over the microphone, and gripped Kurtz's shoulder with his other hand. Kurtz's moan was brief, but the detective kept his hand over the mike. "You're going to go all the way down for this, Kurtz. We have your name in her appointment book. We have a caller who ID'd you at the scene."

Kurtz sighed. "You know I didn't do this, Hathaway. Not my style. When I want to butcher housewives, I always use a Mac 10."

Hathaway showed his big teeth and squeezed harder. This time, Kurtz knew that it was coming and did not moan aloud, even when it seemed that his collarbones were clicking like castanets.

"Take this piece of shit out of here," said Hathaway.

On cue, two huge uniformed officers entered the room, unlocked Kurtz's cuffs, recuffed him with his hands behind his back, and led him out of the room.

One of the uniformed cops had brought a wad of paper towels to dab at the blood dripping from Kurtz's cheek and chin.

Kurtz looked down at his blue oxford-cloth shirt—his only shirt. *Damn.*

The uniforms led him down the hall, through various green corridors, through security checkpoints, downstairs to the basement area where he was finger-printed, searched again, and digitally photographed.

Kurtz knew the drill. With the backlog, it would probably be late the next day before they got around to arraigning him. Kurtz shook his head—Hathaway couldn't be serious about going for Murder One. At the arraignment, for whatever the hell he was actually going to be charged with, Kurtz could post bail and go free until his preliminary hearing.

"What are you smiling at, scumbag?" asked the cop busy trying hard to throw away the huge wad of bloody paper towels without getting any blood on his bare hands.

Kurtz assumed his normal expression. The thought of bail had amused him. Everything he had in the world was in his billfold—a little less than $20. Arlene had been stretched pretty thin, what with fronting the money for the computers and office junk. No, he'd have to sit this one out—first here at the courthouse holding pen, and then down out at the Erie County Jail—until someone in the district attorney's office noticed that there was no case here, that Hathaway was just blowing smoke.

Well, Kurtz judged, he had gotten pretty good at sitting and waiting.

CHAPTER 13

"You understand, my man?" said Malcolm Kibunte to Doo-Rag for the fourth time. "He go up to 'raignment tomorrow sometime, they probably transfer him tomorrow late or next day morning, and he go into general population out at County."

"I unnerstand," said Doo-Rag, beginning to nod a bit, his heavy-lidded gaze becoming a bit more unfocused, but still there enough for Malcolm's purposes.

"Good," said Malcolm and patted the banger on the back.

"What I don't unnerstand, you know, what I need to axe you," said Doo-Rag, squinting through his nod, "is how come, you know, you be getting so fucking generous in your ol' age, Malcolm? You know what I mean? How come you turn over the whole D-Mosque ten bills to me and mine when we do this, you know, this pasty honky fucker for you? You hear what I'm saying?"

Malcolm opened his palms. "It's not for me, Doo. It the Block D-Mosque brothers who want him shanked. No way I can get in there after the dude, so I just pass the word to you, my man. You want to give me some of the *re*-ward, that's cool, but no way I can get myself in there *after* the fucker, hear me? So if your people do the job—" Malcolm shrugged— "fucker's dead, Mosque brothers happy, everything cool."

Doo-Rag was still frowning, working the thing through his drugged mind, but he obviously could not find a catch. "Tomorrow visiting day at County," he said. "Get in early, like ten, pass the word to Lloyd and Small Pee and Daryll, your whiteboy be dead meat before lockdown."

"He may not be transferred until day *after* tomorrow," Malcolm reminded him. "But probably tomorrow. Arraigned tomorrow, probably bussed tomorrow."

"Whenever," said Doo-Rag.

"You got his mug shot, my man?"

Doo-Rag patted the chest pocket of his filthy Desert Storm camouflage jacket.

"You remember his name, my man?"

"Curtis."

"Kurtz," said Malcolm, tapping Doo-Rag's nodding head right on the red do-rag. "Kurtz."

"Whatever," said Doo-Rag, shaking his head and climbing out of the SLK. He sauntered down the avenue, several of his fellow gangbangers falling into the same ambling pace with him. Doo-Rag reached into his baggy trousers, pulled out some of the crack bottles Malcolm had given him, and distributed them to his pals like candy.

CHAPTER 14

Kurtz had almost forgotten how chaotically insane the city holding pens were compared to the regimented insanity of real cellblock life. The lights were on all night and new prisoners were being dragged through in greater numbers as the night grew later; there were already a dozen men in his cell by midnight, and the noise and stink were enough to drive a Buddhist monk bugfuck. One of the junkies was shouting and crying and vomiting and shouting some more until Kurtz went over and helped him relax with two fingers to the nerve that ran along his carotid artery. None of the guards came by to clean up the vomit.

There were three whites in the cell, counting the now-unconscious junkie, and the blacks were doing their usual territorial things and shooting cutting stares and glances Kurtz's way. If any of them recognized him, he knew, they would also know about the D-Mosque *fatwah* and it could mean a long night. There was nothing that Kurtz could use as a weapon—no spring, paper clip, ballpoint—nothing sharp at all, so he decided to just set up an early-warning system and try to get some sleep. Kurtz tossed the slumped junkie off one of the four small benches and used the side of his palm to convince the other white prisoner to sleep on the floor as well. Then Kurtz stacked up their slumped forms as a sort of fence about a yard from the bench. It wouldn't take much effort for the blacks to get over his little roadblock, but it would certainly slow them down a bit. Of course, Kurtz was not discriminating against the African-American prisoners, it was just that there were more of them, and they were more likely to have heard of the bounty.

Cockroaches skittered across the floor, feasted on the pool of vomit in no-man's-land, and then explored the folds of the junkie's clothes and crawled across the other white guy's exposed ankle.

Kurtz curled up on the unpadded bench and went into a half doze, eyes closed, but his face toward the mass of other men. After a while, their murmuring died down, and most of them dozed or sat cursing. Cops dragged whores and junkies past the cell toward the next corridor of pens. Evidently, this inn had not yet put out its No Vacancy sign for the night.

Sometime around 2:00 A.M., Kurtz snapped fully awake and pulled his fist far back in a killing mode. Movement. It was only a uniformed cop unlocking the cell door.

"Joe Kurtz."

Kurtz went out warily, not turning his back on either the other prisoners or the cop. This might be Hathaway's plan—the throwdown was certainly still around somewhere. Or maybe one of the cops had seen the paperwork on his arrest and connected him with the Death Mosque bounty.

The uniformed cop was fat and sleepy looking and—like all of the cops in the cell corridor—had left his weapon on the other side of the main sliding grate. The cop carried a baton in his hand and a can of Mace on his belt. Video cameras followed their movement. Kurtz decided that if Hathaway or anyone else was waiting around the bend in the corridor, about all he could do was take the baton away from the fat cop, use him as a shield during any shooting, and try to get in close. It was a shitty plan, but the best he could improvise without access to another weapon.

No one was waiting around the corridor. They passed through the doors and grates without incident. In the booking room another sleepy sergeant returned his wallet, keys, and change in a brown envelope and then led him up the back stairs to the main hall. There they unlocked the cage and let him walk.

A beautiful brunette—full-breasted, long-haired, with lovely skin and alluring eyes—was sitting on a long bench in the filthy waiting area. She got up when he came out. Kurtz wondered idly how anyone could look so fresh and put together at two in the morning.

"Mr. Kurtz, you look like shit," said the brunette.

Kurtz nodded.

"Mr. Kurtz, my name is—"

"Sophia Farino," said Kurtz. "Little Skag showed me a picture of you."

She smiled slightly. "The family calls him 'Stephen.' "

"Everyone else who's met him calls him 'Little Skag' or just 'Skag,' " said Kurtz.

Sophia Farino nodded. "Shall we go?"

Kurtz stood where he was. "You're telling me that you made bail for me?"

She nodded.

"Why you?" said Kurtz. "If the family wanted it done, why not send Miles the lawyer down? And why in the middle of the night? Why not wait for the arraignment?"

"There never was going to be any arraignment," said Sophia. "You were going to be charged with parole violations—carrying a firearm—and sent over to County in the morning."

Kurtz rubbed his chin and heard the stubble rasp. "Parole violation?"

Sophia smiled and began walking. Kurtz followed her down the echoing stairway and out into the night. He was very alert, his nerves pulled very tight. Without being obvious about it, he was checking every shadow, responding to every movement.

"The Richardson murder has lots of clues," said Sophia, "but none of them lead to you. They already have a blood type from the semen they found on the woman. Not yours."

"How do you know?"

Instead of answering, she said, "Someone made an anonymous call that you were at the Richardson place yesterday. If they told you that the woman had your name in her Day-Timer, they lied. She'd scribbled something about meeting a Mr. Quotes."

"The lady was never very good with names," said Kurtz.

Sophia led the way out into the cold but brilliantly lighted parking lot and beeped a black Porsche Boxster open. "Want a ride?" she said.

"I'll walk," said Kurtz.

"Not wise," said the woman. "You know why someone went to all this work to get you to County?"

Kurtz did, of course. At least now he did. A yard hit. A shank job. He was lucky that it hadn't happened in interrogation or the holding pen. Hathaway almost certainly had been part of the setup. What had kept the homicide cop from going ahead with it, using the throwdown and the Glock, and collecting the ten grand? His young partner? Kurtz would probably never know. But he was sure that someone else would have been waiting downstream and that Hathaway would still have gotten his cut.

"You'd better ride with me," said Sophia.

"How do I know you're not the one?" said Kurtz.

Don Farino's daughter laughed. It was a rich, unselfconscious laugh, her head thrown back, a totally sincere laugh from a grown-up woman. "You flatter me," she said. "I have something to talk to you about, Kurtz, and this would be a good time. I think I can help you figure out who's setting you up for this hit and why. Last offer. Want a ride?"

Kurtz went around and got in the passenger side of the low, muscular Boxster.

CHAPTER 15

Kurtz had expected either just a ride and a talk or a trip out to the Farino family manse in Orchard Park, but Sophia drove him to her loft in the old section of downtown Buffalo.

He knew that she'd had to pass through a metal detector even to get into the waiting area of the city jail, so there was no weapon in the purse she tossed on the floor of the Boxster's passenger side. That meant the center console. If the woman had unclicked that console during the short drive, it would have been an interesting few seconds of activity for Kurtz, but she went nowhere near it.

Her loft was in an old warehouse that had been gentrified, given huge windows and metal terraces that looked out toward the downtown or the harbor, had a secure parking lot dug out under the building, and sported security guards in the lobby and basement entrance. *Sort of like my current place,* thought Kurtz with a hint of irony.

Sophia used a security card to get into the parking basement, exchanged pleasantries with the uniformed guard at the door to the elevators, and took Kurtz up to the sixth—and top—floor.

"I'll get us drinks," she said after entering the loft, locking the door behind her, and tossing her keys into an enameled vase on a red-lacquer side table. "Scotch do?"

"Sure," said Kurtz. He had not eaten since a slice of toast that morning—yesterday morning now—about twenty hours earlier.

The don's daughter had a nice place: exposed brick, modern furniture that still looked comfortable, a wide-screen HDTV in one corner with the usual gaggle of stereo equipment—DVD players, VCR, surround-sound receivers, pre-amps. There were tall, framed French minimalist posters that looked original—and which were probably as expensive as hell—a mezzanine under skylights with hundreds of books set in black lacquer shelves, and a huge, semicircular window dominating the west wall with a view of the river, the harbor, and the bridge lights.

She handed him the Scotch. He sipped some. Chivas.

"Aren't you going to compliment me on my place?" she said.

Kurtz shrugged. It would be a great place to hit if he were into robbery, but he doubted if she would take that as a compliment. "You were going to tell me your theories," he said.

Sophia sipped her Scotch and sighed. "Come here, Kurtz," she said, not actually touching him on the arm, but leading him over to a full-length mirror near the door. "What do you see?" she asked after she stepped back.

"Me," said Kurtz. In truth, he saw a hollow-eyed man with matted hair, a torn, bloodied shirt, a fresh scratch along one cheek, and rivulets of dried blood on his face and neck.

"You stink, Kurtz."

He nodded, taking the comment in the spirit it was meant—a statement of fact.

"You need to take a shower," she said. "Get into some clean clothes."

"Later," he said. There was no warm water and no clean clothes at his warehouse flop.

"Now," said Sophia and took his Scotch glass and set it on the counter. She went into a bathroom in the short hall between the living room and what looked like a bedroom. Kurtz heard water running. She poked her head out into the hall. "Coming?"

"No," said Kurtz.

"Jesus, you're paranoid."

Yeah, thought Kurtz, *but am I paranoid enough?*

Sophia had kicked off her shoes and now was pulling off her blouse and skirt. She wore only white underpants and a white bra. With a motion that Kurtz had not seen in person in more than eleven years, she unhooked the bra and tossed it out of sight. She stood there in her white, lacy but not trampy underpants, cut high on the sides. "Well?" she said.

. Kurtz checked the door. Bolted and police locked. He checked the small kitchen. Another door, bolted and chained. He slid open the door to the terrace and walked out onto the metal structure. It was cold and beginning to rain. There was no way to gain access to the terrace short of rappelling from the rooftop. He went back in, walked past Sophia—who had her arms crossed in front of her full breasts but who was still goose-bumpy from the sudden blast of cold air—and checked the bedroom, looking into the closets and under the bed.

Then he came back to the bathroom.

Sophia was naked now, standing under the warm water, her long, curly hair already wet. "My God," she said through the open shower door, "you *are* paranoid."

Kurtz took off his bloody clothes.

Kurtz was excited, but not crazy excited. After the first couple of years without sex, he had realized, the need for it stayed the same but the obsession for it either drove men crazy—he had seen plenty of that in Attica—or leveled off to a sort of metaphysical hunger. Kurtz had read Epictetus and the other Stoics while serving his time and found their philosophy admirable but boring. The trick, he thought, was to enjoy the hard-on but not be led around by it.

Sophia soaped him all over, not neglecting his erection. She was very gentle when cleaning his face, making sure not to get soap into the cuts there.

"I don't think you'll need stitches," she said and then her eyes widened a bit as he began soaping her— not just her breasts and pubic hair, but her neck, face, back, shoulders, arms, and legs. Evidently, she had expected a bit more straightforward approach.

She reached up to what looked like a covered soap dish on the tile ledge, removed a condom packet, tore it open with her teeth, and slid the rubber onto Kurtz's stiffened penis. He smiled at her efficiency but wasn't in need of the protection quite yet. Kurtz pulled the shampoo off the same ledge and lathered it into the woman's long hair, rubbing her skull and temples with strong fingers. Sophia closed her eyes a minute and then found the shampoo bottle, rubbing the liquid into his short hair. The top of her head came just about to nose level on Kurtz and she raised her face to kiss him after they rinsed the shampoo off and let it flow down their bodies. His penis rubbed against the soft curve of her belly and she held the back of his neck with her left hand while her right hand went lower to grip and massage him.

She pushed against him, raising one leg high as she leaned back against the tile. Kurtz rinsed the soap and shampoo from her breasts and tasted her nipples. His right hand was set against the small of her back while his left hand gently massaged her vulva. He felt her thighs tremble and then open wider and then the heat from her poured into his cupped palm. His fingers probed gently. It was still amazing to Kurtz that they could be in a pounding shower and that a woman could be palpably *wetter* there than anywhere else.

"Please, now," she whispered, her mouth wet and open against his cheek. "Now."

They moved together hard. Kurtz made his right hand a saddle and lifted her higher against the tiles while she wrapped her legs around his hips and leaned back, her hands cusped behind his neck, her arm and thigh muscles straining.

When she came it was with a low moan and a fluttering of eyelids, but also with a spasm that he could feel through the head of his cock, his thighs, and splayed fingers of his supporting hand.

"Jesus Christ," she whispered in a moment, still being held against the tile in the warm spray. Kurtz wondered just how capacious this loft's hot water tank was. After another moment, she kissed him, began moving again, and said, "I didn't feel you come. Don't you want to come?"

"Later," said Kurtz and lifted her slightly. She moaned again when he slid out of her and she cupped his balls while his erection throbbed against her pubic hair.

"My God," she said, smiling now, "you'd think it was *me* who'd been in jail for a dozen years."

"Eleven and a half," said Kurtz. He turned off the shower and they toweled each other off. The towels were thick and fluffy.

As she rubbed between his legs, she said, "You're still hard as ever. How can you stand it?"

In answer, Kurtz lifted her and carried her into her bedroom.

CHAPTER 16

It was after 5:00 A.M. when they finally separated and lay next to each other on the bed that Kurtz had decided was exactly the size of his former cell.

Sophia lit a cigarette and offered him one. Kurtz shook his head.

"A con who doesn't smoke," she said. "Unheard of."

"Watching TV from the inside," he said, "you get the impression that everyone on the outside has given up smoking and is busy suing the tobacco companies. Guess it ain't so."

"Say it ain't so, Joe," said Sophia. She set a small enamel ashtray on her sheeted belly and flicked ashes. "So, Joe Kurtz," she said, "why did you come to my father with this private-investigation bullshit?"

"It wasn't bullshit. It's what I do."

Sophia exhaled smoke and shook her head. "I mean the offer to find Buell Richardson. You must know as well as I do that he's in Lake Erie or under four feet of loam somewhere."

"Yeah."

"Then why offer to find him and haul him back for a bonus?"

Kurtz rubbed his eyes. He was feeling a bit sleepy. "Seemed like a way to get work."

"A lot of effort you've spent on the job so far. Went to visit Buell's widow—who got herself killed as soon as you left, it sounds like—and crippled our poor, late Carl."

"Late?" Kurtz was surprised. "He's dead?"

"Some complications in the hospital," said Sophia. "What did Skag tell you about the truck hijackings and Richardson's disappearance?"

"Enough to let me know that it's more complicated than it looks," said Kurtz. "Someone's either moving in on your father, or there's something else in play here."

"Any suspects?" asked Sophia, stubbing out her cigarette and looking directly at Kurtz. The sheet had slipped from her breasts and she made no effort to pull it back in place.

"Sure," said Kurtz. "Miles the lawyer, of course. Any of your father's top guys who are getting ambitious."

"All the ambitious ones left since Papa retired."

"Yeah, I know," said Kurtz.

"So that leaves Miles."

"And you."

Sophia did not feign outrage. "Sure. But why would I be pulling this crap when I inherit Papa's money, anyway?"

"Good question," said Kurtz. "Now it's my turn. You said that you could tell me who's setting me up for a hit."

Sophia shook her head. "I don't know for sure, but if Miles is involved, you might watch out for a guy named Malcolm Kibunte and a scary white friend of his."

"Malcolm Kibunte," Kurtz repeated. "Don't know him. Description?"

"Former Crip from Philadelphia. Big, black, mean as a snake-bit Mormon. Early thirties. Shaves his head, but wears one of those little major-league-pitcher goatees. Wears black leather and lots of jewelry. Has a diamond stud in his front tooth. I've seen him only once. I don't think Leonard Miles knows that I know about their contacts."

"I won't ask how you know," said Kurtz.

Sophia lit another cigarette, took a long drag and exhaled smoke and said nothing.

"What's our Malcolm friend into?" said Kurtz.

"He left Philly one step ahead of a murder rap," said Sophia. "Not for the Crips, though. Popped a cap on a fellow Crip for one of the Colombian rings down there. Malcolm was into moving coke big time. Then he began specializing on eliminating competitors."

"Served time?" said Kurtz.

"Nothing serious. Aggravated assault. Illegal possession of a weapon. Killed his first wife—strangled her."

"That must have cost him some time."

"Not much. Miles represented him and got him two years on a psychiatric thing. I think that's why Miles thinks that Kibunte is on a leash. I wouldn't bet my life on it if I were Miles."

"And what about this white friend of his?"

Sophia shook her head. Her curly hair was dry and curlier than ever. "Haven't seen him. Don't have a name. Supposed to be real white—almost albino—and good with a blade."

"Ahh," said Kurtz.

"Ah, indeed." Sophia sighed. "If Papa were still in charge of things in Buffalo, these two would have been swatted like flies as soon as they showed up in town. But I doubt if Papa has even heard of them."

"Why exactly did your father get squeezed out of the local action?"

Sophia sighed. "Did Skag tell you about the shooting?"

"Just the fact of it, not the details."

"Well, it's simple enough," said Sophia. "About eight years ago, Papa and two of his bodyguards were driving back from a restaurant down in Boston Hills when a couple of cars tried to block them in. Papa's driver was well trained, of course, and the glass was bulletproof, but when the driver was backing out of the trap they'd set, one of the shooters used a shotgun on the driver's-side window, shattered it, and then sprayed the inside with automatic weapons' fire. Papa was just scratched, but both his men were killed."

She paused and flicked ashes into the enamel ashtray.

"So Papa crawled over the seat, took the wheel, and drove that Caddy out of there himself," she continued, "returning fire with Lester's—the driver's—nine-millimeter. He got at least one of the shooters."

"Were they white or black?" asked Kurtz.

"White," said Sophia. "Anyway, Papa would have gotten away all right, but someone used a .357 Magnum to fire through the trunk of the Caddy. The damned slug went through the rear end, the spare tire, both seats, and ended up in Papa's back, a quarter of an inch from his spine. And that trunk was *armored*."

"Did Don Farino figure out who'd put the hit on him?"

Sophia shrugged. Her nipples were a delicate brown. "A lot of inquiries, a few suspects, but no confirmation. It was probably the Gonzagas."

"They're the only other Italian mob with action in western New York, right?" said Kurtz.

Sophia frowned. "We don't call them 'Italian mob.'"

"Okay," said Kurtz. "The Gonzagas are the only other guinea gangsters licensed to do business in this end of the state, right?"

"Right."

"And it's been about six years since what's left of the Farinos had any real clout?"

"Yes," she said. "Things went downhill after Papa was crippled."

Kurtz nodded. "Your oldest brother, David, tried to keep the family in the action until the mid-90's. Then he killed himself in a car accident while coked to the eyes, and your older sister took off for a nunnery in Italy."

Sophia nodded.

"And then Little Skag fucked things up for a while until the other families decided it was time for your father to retire," said Kurtz. "Little Skag gets high and attacks his Brazilian girlfriend with a shovel, and here you are, alone in that big house with Papa."

Sophia said nothing.

"What's being hijacked?" asked Kurtz. "On the trucks they hit?"

"VCRs, DVD players, cigarettes," said Sophia. "The usual penny-ante crap. The New York families are big into bootleg videos and DVDs, and that means they've got thousands of machines to unload. They toss Papa that crumb. The cigarettes are just for old times' sake."

"Untaxed cigarettes can bring in nice money," said Kurtz.

"Not in the quantities that they let our family have," said Sophia. She slid out of bed and walked to the closet. There was a thick robe on one of the leather chairs by the window, but she ignored it, obviously feeling comfortable naked. "You're going to have to get out of here," she said. "It's almost sunrise."

Kurtz nodded and got out of bed.

"My God, you've got a lot of scars," said Sophia Farino.

"Accident prone," said Kurtz. "Where are my clothes?"

"Down the disposal chute," she said. She slid back one of the mirrored doors and took a man's denim shirt, some packaged Jockey shorts, and a pair of corduroy trousers out of a drawer. "Take these," she said. "They should fit you. I'll get some new sneakers and socks for you."

Kurtz tossed the shirt back. "Don't wear these," he said.

"Don't wear what?" she said. "Shirts? Denim shirts?"

"Polo ponies."

"You're shitting me. That's a brand-new two-hundred-dollar shirt."

Kurtz shrugged. "I don't wear company logos. If they want me to advertise for them, they can pay me."

Sophia Farino laughed again and once again Kurtz enjoyed the sound of it. "A man of principle," she said. "Butchered Eddie Falco, crippled ol' Carl, and shot God knows how many others in cold blood, but a man of principle. I love it." She tossed him a cheaper-looking denim shirt. "No ponies, alligators, sheep, Nike swooshes, or anything else on it. Satisfied?"

Kurtz pulled it on. It fit fine. So did the underpants, corduroy slacks, socks, and boat shoes. He didn't think that Sophia had gone shopping ahead of time for him, so he wondered how many men's sizes she kept in stock. Maybe it was like the package of condoms in the shower: *Be prepared* was evidently this woman's motto. He headed for the front door.

"Hey," she said, finally pulling on the robe and padding along beside him. "It's cold out there."

"Did you throw away my jacket as well?"

"Damned right I did." She opened the foyer closet door and handed him an expensive, insulated leather bomber jacket. "This should fit you."

It did. He unbolted the door.

"Kurtz," she said. "You're still naked." She took a 9mm Sig Sauer from the closet and offered it to him.

Kurtz checked it—the magazine was fully loaded—and then handed it back. "Don't know where it's been," he said.

Sophia smiled. "It's not traceable. Don't you trust me?"

Kurtz twitched a smile and let her keep the pistol. He went out the door, down a private hallway, took the elevator to the ground floor, and went out into the dark past a sleepy but curious front-lobby security guard. When he'd walked a block west, he looked back at the loft building. Her lights were still on, but they flicked out as he watched.

CHAPTER 17

Kurtz's current bolthole was in an old icehouse being renovated into lofts, but it was a mile or so from the already-gentrified area where Sophia Farino had her pied-à-terre. It was not really light yet, but there was a certain brighter grayness to the low clouds that were drizzling on him.

He felt naked without a weapon, and a little woozy. He put that down to not having eaten or drunk anything except the glass of Chivas for the past twenty-four hours rather than because of great sex. Kurtz admitted to himself that he'd had images of sitting around in those soft terry-cloth robes, enjoying a huge breakfast of bacon and eggs and steaming hot coffee with Ms. Farino before he headed out into the storm. *Getting soft, Joe,* he thought. At least the expensive bomber jacket was warm against the icy drizzle.

Kurtz was walking under the I-90 overpass when a memory struck him. He left the sidewalk, climbed the steep concrete gradient, and peered into the low, dark niches where the concrete supports met iron girders. The first two cubbies were empty except for pigeon crap and human shit, but the third held a small skeletal figure that pulled back to the far end of the cluttered hole. As Kurtz's eyes adapted to the dark, he could make out wide white eyes, trembling shoulders, and long, bare, quaking arms emerging from a torn T-shirt. Even in the dim light, he could see the bruises and track marks on those arms. The thin man tried to pull himself farther back from the opening.

"Hey, it's okay, Pruno," said Kurtz. He reached out and patted the arm. It was almost fleshless and colder than some corpses Kurtz had handled. "It's me, Joe Kurtz."

"Joseph?" said the quaking figure. "Really you, Joseph?"

"Yeah."

"When'd you get out?"

"Just a while ago."

Pruno came farther out and tried to smooth out the flattened cardboard box and stinking blanket he was sitting on. The rest of the niche was filled with bottles and newspapers that the man obviously had been using for insulation.

"Where the hell's your sleeping bag, Pruno?"

"Somebody stole it, Joseph. Just a couple nights ago. I think . . . it wasn't long ago. Just when it was turning cold."

"You should go to the shelter, man."

Pruno lifted one of the bottles of wine and offered it. Kurtz shook his head. "Shelter's getting meaner every year," said the wino and junkie. "Work for sleep's the motto now."

"Working's better than freezing to death," said Kurtz.

Pruno shrugged. "I'll find a better blanket when one of the old street guys dies. 'Round about first snow, probably. So how are the guys in C Block, Joseph?"

"Last year they moved me to D Block," said Kurtz. "But I heard that Billy the C went to L.A. when he got out and is working in the movies out there."

"Acting?"

"Providing set security."

Pruno made a sound that started as a laugh and soon turned into a cough. "Usual protection racket. Those movie guys eat it up. What about you, Joseph? Heard that the Mosque brothers were pronouncing *fatwah* on you, as if they knew what that meant."

Kurtz shrugged. "Most people know that the D-bros don't have the money for that. I'm not worried. Hey, Pruno—you know anything about some Farino trucks being knocked over?"

The haggard, bearded figure looked up from his bottle. "You working for the Farinos these days, Joseph?"

"Not really. Just doing what I used to do."

"What do you want to know about the trucks?"

"Who's hitting them. When is the next job due?"

Pruno closed his eyes. The light was coming up gray beyond the overpass, and illuminated the filthy, haggard face enough to remind Kurtz of carved wooden statues of Jesus he had seen in Mexico. "I think I heard something about a low-rent type named Doo-Rag and his boys fencing some cigarettes and DVD players after the last truck thing," said Pruno. "No one tells me about crimes in the planning stage."

"Doo-Rag the Blood?" said Kurtz.

"Yes. You know him?"

Kurtz shook his head. "There was a punk in D Block got shanked in the showers supposedly because he owed money to a young Blood named Doo-Rag. Supposedly this Doo-Rag played a season for the NBA."

"Nonsense," said Pruno, emphasizing both syllables. "Closest Doo-Rag got to the NBA was the public courts up at Delaware Park."

"Those are pretty good," said Kurtz. "Would a Blood like Doo-Rag take marching orders from an ex-Crip?"

Pruno coughed again. "Everyone is doing business with everyone these days, Joseph. It's the global economy. You ever see a brochure from any of those top Ivy League—type colleges the last ten years or so?"

"No," said Kurtz. "I haven't received too many of those." He knew that Pruno had been a college professor at one time.

"Diversity and tolerance," said Pruno and drank the last of his wine. "Tolerance and diversity. No mention of the canon, of the classics, of knowledge or learning. Just tolerance and diversity and diversity and tolerance. It paves the way for global e-commerce and personal empowerment." His rheumy eyes focused on Kurtz in the dim light. "Yes, Joseph, Doo-Rag and his street associates would take orders from an ex-Crip if it meant money. Then they'd try to kill the motherfucker. Which ex-Crip are we talking about?"

"Malcolm Kibunte."

Pruno shrugged and then began shivering again. "Didn't know Malcolm Kibunte was ever a Crip."

"You know of any arrangements between this Malcolm or Doo-Rag and the Farinos?"

Pruno coughed again. "Doesn't seem likely, since the Farinos are as racist as all the rest of the wiseguy families. To be more succinct, Joseph—no."

"Know where I can find Kibunte?"

"I don't. But I'll ask around."

"Don't be too obvious about it, Pruno."

"Never, Joseph."

"One more question. Do you know anything about a white guy that this Malcolm hangs around with?"

"Cutter?" Pruno's voice was quaking from the cold or withdrawal.

"That's his name?"

"That is what people know him as, Joseph. I know nothing else. I wish to know nothing else. A very disturbed individual, Joseph. Please stay clear of him."

Kurtz nodded. "You need to get to a shelter and at least get a decent blanket, Pruno. Some food. Spend some time with people. Don't you get lonely out here?"

"*Numquam se minus otiosum esse, quam cum otiosus, nec minus solum, quam cum solus esset,*" said the junkie. "Are you familiar with Seneca, Joseph? I had him on your reading list."

"Haven't got that far yet, I guess," said Kurtz. "Seneca the Indian chief?"

"No, Joseph, although he was quite eloquent as well. Especially after we whites gave his people a 'gift' of blankets riddled with smallpox. No, Seneca the philosopher. . . ." Pruno's eyes grew vague and lost.

"You want to translate for me?" said Kurtz. "Like old times?"

Pruno smiled. "*That he was never less idle than when he was idle, and never less alone than when he was alone.* Seneca attributed it to Scipio Africanus, Joseph."

Kurtz took his leather jacket off and set it on Pruno's lap.

"I can't accept this, Joseph."

"It was a freebie," said Kurtz. "Got it less than an hour ago. I've got a closet full of those things at home."

"Bullshit, Joseph. Absolute bullshit."

Kurtz tapped the old man on his bony shoulder and slid down the embankment. He wanted to get back to his warehouse before it was truly light.

CHAPTER 18

The old, seven-story brick building had been built as an icehouse, then served as a warehouse through most of the twentieth century, then made money as a U-Store-It warehouse for a couple of decades with its grand old spaces broken up into a warren of cages and windowless cells. Most recently, it had been bought by a consortium of lawyers who were going to make a killing by converting it to expensive condo-lofts opening onto city views on the outside with interior mezzanines looking down into a fancy center atrium. The architect's prospectus had used Los Angeles's Bradbury Building, that favorite location interior for TV shows and films, as a template: clean brick, fancy ironwork, interior iron stairways and cage elevators, dozens of offices with frosted glass doors. Developers had begun the conversion: fencing off the entire structure, leaving the central section open as the atrium, adding rough mezzanines on the upper floors, adding an expensive skylight, knocking down some walls, cutting out some windows. But the loft market had slowed down, the gentrification had crept in the opposite direction, the lawyers' money had dried up, and now the warehouse sat alone except for the dozen other abandoned brick warehouses around it. The lawyers, ever optimistic, had left some of the construction materials at the fenced-off site in anticipation of getting back to work on it as soon as the consortium came into new funds.

Doc, the gun salesman/nightwatchman in Lackawanna, had mentioned the place to Kurtz. Doc had actually guarded the site for a while a year before, when hopes for the return of money and work were higher. Kurtz liked what he heard about it: electrical power had been restored for the upper two floors and the elevator, although the bottom floors were still a lightless, windowless maze of narrow corridors and metal cages walled off from the atrium. A private security service dropped by the place two or three times a week, but only to make sure that the fence was intact and the padlocks and chains secure.

Kurtz had cut through the fence at the least convenient part of the perimeter—back where the property ran along the rail lines—and had used the combination Doc had provided for the five-number padlock on the rear door. The window on that door had been conveniently broken before Kurtz first arrived, so it was no problem leaning out to click the padlock shut and scramble the combination.

Kurtz had approved of the place immediately. It wasn't heated—which would be a problem when the Buffalo winter arrived in earnest—but there was running water on the seventh floor for some of the construction sinks there. One of the three huge service elevators still worked, although Kurtz never took it. The sound it made reminded him of the monster's roar in the old *Godzilla* movies. There was a wide staircase off the front hallway that let light through thick glass blocks, a windowless interior stairway in the back, and two sets of rusting fire escapes. A few windows had been carved out on the top two floors, but no glass had been put in.

The bottom three floors were a lightless, littered mess except for the echoing atrium, which was a sky-lighted, littered mess. The atrium offered an avenue of retreat if one were bold enough to trust the scaffolding that ran up the interior all the way to the skylight. The consortium had just got to the sandblasting-interior-brick stage when the money ran out.

This morning, Kurtz shivered a bit in the cold rain as he walked down the rusted tracks, slipped through the cut in the fence and rearranged the wire so that the hole was invisible, let himself in the back way, checked telltales he had left in the lobby hallway, and then jogged up the five flights of the front stairway.

He had made a nest for himself on the sixth floor. The room was small and windowless—all of the storage rooms had been set up between the outer hall and the atrium wall—but Kurtz had run an extension cord through the crumbling ceiling and rigged a trouble light. He'd set up a cot with a decent sleeping bag—

borrowed from Arlene—and had his leaving-Attica gym bag, a flashlight, and a few books on the floor. He kept both weapons oiled and ready and wrapped in oil rags in the gym bag, along with a cheap sweatsuit he'd picked up for pajamas. This particular cubby actually had a bathroom—or at least a toilet added sometime in the 1920s when the place was still an icehouse with offices—and Kurtz sometimes hauled water down from the seventh floor. The plumbing worked, but there was no bath or shower.

It was a pain in the ass climbing the five flights of stairs day and night, but what Kurtz liked about the place was the acoustics—the hallways amplified sound so that footsteps could be heard two flights above, the elevator—which he had tried—could wake the dead, and the atrium was like a giant echo chamber. It would be very hard for someone new to the space to sneak up on anyone familiar with it.

Also, Kurtz had discovered, between the century and a half of use and the recent renovations, there were a multitude of nooks, crannies, niches, ladders, walled-off rooms, and other hiding places. He had spent time exploring these with a good flashlight. And—best of all—there was an old tunnel which ran from the basement several hundred yards east to another old warehouse.

Kurtz looked in the carton he thought of as his refrigerator. Two bottles of water and a few Oreos were left. He ate the Oreos and drank an entire bottle of water. He crawled into his sleeping bag and glanced at his watch: 6:52 A.M. He had planned to go into the office this morning to work with Arlene, but he could be a little late.

Kurtz clicked off the trouble light, curled up in the near-absolute darkness, waited a bit for his shivering to abate as the bag warmed up, and drifted off to sleep.

"Got him," said Malcolm Kibunte. He and Cutter were in an AstroVan parked almost two blocks away.

It had been a long night. When the courthouse cop on the arm informed Miles that someone had made bail for Kurtz, Malcolm let Doo-Rag know that the yard shank was off, gathered Cutter, his Tek-9, and some surveillance gear, stole a van, and staked out the jail. The revised plan was to take out Kurtz in a rock-and-roll drive-by the minute he got out of ricochet range of the city jail, killing him and whoever had made the bail for him. Then Malcolm saw who it was who had posted bail, and went to Plan Three.

They waited down the street from Sophia Farino's condo through the early-morning hours and were almost ready to bag it when Kurtz finally emerged and began strolling the opposite way. There were so few vehicles on the street that Malcolm had to let Kurtz disappear from sight and then drive in long loops to get ahead of him, always parked with other grimy vans and vehicles, always a good two blocks away. It was dark. Only the expensive military night scopes and goggles allowed Cutter and Malcolm to keep tabs on Kurtz.

For a while they thought they had run him to ground when Kurtz had clambered up under the expressway overpass, but just as Malcolm and Cutter were getting ready to go after him, Kurtz climbed down the embankment and was on the move again. For some reason, the fool had ditched his jacket. Cutter wanted to stop under the overpass and check on that, but Malcolm was too busy driving down toward the river and finding a place to park before Kurtz wandered into sight again. It was getting light. Surveillance would be impossible in half an hour or so: Kurtz would notice the same scabrous green van if it kept reappearing, even a couple of blocks away.

But luck was with them. From where they had parked in an old railroad salvage-yard, Malcolm watched through the night-vision scope, and Cutter lifted the huge binoculars as Kurtz went through his slice in the wire and let himself into the old icehouse building.

They waited another hour. Kurtz did not come out.

"I think we found his hidey-hole," said Malcolm. He rubbed his beard and lifted the Tek-9 onto his lap. Cutter grunted and clicked open his knife. "I don't know, C, my man," said Malcolm. "Big place in there. Probably dark. He know it, we don't."

The two sat in silence for another few minutes. Suddenly Malcolm grinned broadly. "You know what we need for this job, C?"

Cutter looked at him, his pale eyes empty.

"That's right," said Malcolm. "We gonna need extreme white trash, stupid enough not to know about the Death Mosque bounty, but still be willin' to go in there to kill Mr. Kurtz for next to nothing."

Cutter nodded.

"Correct," agreed Malcolm. "We know where Mr. Kurtz live. All we need to do now is bring in the Alabama Beagle Boys." Malcolm laughed heartily.

Cutter breathed through his mouth and turned to look at the old icehouse through the rain.

CHAPTER 19

"Nice couch," said Kurtz as Arlene came down the back steps and into their basement office. He was half-asleep, sprawled on the sprung, faded floral sofa. "Is it from your house?"

"Nice of you to drop by and notice," said Arlene, hanging her coat on a spike driven into the wall. "Of course it's from the house. Alan slept through many an NFL game on it. I had Will and Bobby help me haul it down here. What is this on my desk?"

"A video monitor," said Kurtz.

"A TV?"

"Go ahead, turn it on."

Arlene flicked it on and looked at the picture for a minute. It was fuzzy and in black and white and cycled through four scenes: counter, stacks, booths, and hallway. "That's it? I get to watch the perverts in the porn shop upstairs?"

"That's it," agreed Kurtz. "The owners revamped the closed-circuit surveillance system upstairs, and I got Jimmy to run a line down here and sell us one of the old monitors."

"*Sell* it to us?" Arlene tapped the mouse to bring her computer screen to life. "How much did it cost?"

"Fifty bucks, wiring thrown in free. I told him I'd pay when I got the money this month . . . or next . . . or whenever."

"Just so I can watch the dirty old men buying their dirty old magazines and videos."

"You're welcome," said Kurtz. He swung himself off the sprung couch and walked over to his own desk at the rear of the long room. His desk was empty, except for some files and memos left there by Arlene.

"Do you really think we need the video security?" she asked. "Both doors stay locked and we're not exactly advertising that we're here."

Kurtz shrugged. "The outer door's pretty well jimmy-proof," he said. "But the door from the porn shop is just a door. And I seem to have a few people hunting for me." He poured coffee for both of them, even though Arlene had just come in from her lunch break, carried the mugs over, and sat on the edge of her desk. He gave her Pruno's description of Malcolm Kibunte, Cutter, and Doo-Rag, then remembered Sammy Levine's brother Manny and described him as well.

"You made an enemy out of Danny DeVito?" said Arlene.

"Sounds like it," said Kurtz. "Anyway, if you see anyone on the monitor who looks like any of these four guys upstairs, you leave by one of the other doors."

"Those descriptions apply to about half of the losers who patronize the shop upstairs," said Arlene.

"All right," said Kurtz. "Amend it to—if you see anyone trying to bust through the front door up there, you head out the back. If any of them look like one of the guys I described, move even faster."

Arlene nodded. "Any other gifts for me?"

Kurtz pulled the Kimber Custom .45 ACP from the holster at the small of his back. He set it on her desk. "Couldn't afford a Doberman," he said.

Arlene shook her head and reached under her desk, pulling out a hammerless, short-barreled .32 Magnum Ruger revolver.

"Hey," said Kurtz, "an old friend!"

"I thought that if it was going to be like the old days, I'd better act as if it was the old days." She hefted the weapon. "The last few years, the only reason I've had to go out is my weekly mah-jongg at Bernice's and the twice-weekly evenings at the shooting range." She slid the Ruger back into the holstered box screwed to the underside of her desk drawer.

"They didn't let us practice much target shooting inside," said Kurtz. "You're probably a better shot than I am these days."

"I always was," said Arlene.

Hiding his relief at not having to give up the Kimber .45, Kurtz set the semiautomatic back in its concealed-carry holster, removed the holster, and flopped back on the couch.

"Are you interested in how Sweetheart Search, Inc., is doing?" said Arlene. "It is your business, after all. And all the skip-trace sites and services you told me about are working out fine. We pay them, charge the sweetheart wannabe twenty percent more, and everyone's happy. Want to see it in action?"

"Yeah, sure," said Kurtz. "But right now I'm thinking about something I'm working on. You could use it to look up Malcolm Kibunte for me, though. Usual sources—court appearances, warrants, back taxes due, whatever. I know he won't have a real home address, but I'll take whatever you find."

Arlene tapped away at her computer keys for a while, checking that day's hits, processing encrypted credit-card orders for searches, transferring the money to the new account, filing data into her search engines, and then beginning the search for Malcolm Kibunte. Finally she said, "I know you never talk about your cases, but do you want to tell me about what's going on now? There's some scary stuff in here about your Mr. Kibunte."

When Kurtz did not reply, she glanced his way. Sprawled on the couch, the holstered .45 clutched to his chest like a teddy bear, he was beginning to snore.

CHAPTER 20

Blue Franklin was an old blues bar that had only gotten better with age. Young up-and-coming blues stars had played in the smoke haze and platter rattle of the little place on Franklin Street for six decades, gone on to national prominence, and then come back to play to packed houses in their prime and old age. The two playing this night were in their prime: Pearl Wilson, a vocalist in her late thirties who combined a Billie Holiday–like poignancy with a growing Koko Taylor rough edge, and Big Beau Turner, one of the best tenor-sax men since Warne Marsh.

Kurtz came for the late set, nursed a beer, and enjoyed Pearl's interpretation of "Hell Hound on My Trail," "Sweet Home Chicago," "Come in My Kitchen," "Willow, Weep for Me," "Big-Legged Mamas Are Back in Style," and "Run the Voodoo Down," followed by

Big Beau doing solo riffs on a series of Billy Strayhorn pieces: "Blood Count," "Lush Life," "Drawing-Room Blues," and "U.M.M.G."

Kurtz could not remember a time, even as a boy, when he had not loved jazz and blues. It was the closest thing to religion he knew. In jail, even when he'd been allowed access to a Discman or cassette player, which wasn't that much of the time, even a perfect recorded performance such as Miles Davis's remastered "Kind of Blue" had been no substitute for a live performance with its ebb and flow of tidal forces, like a well-played baseball game gone deep into extra innings, now all lethargy and distance, transformed in an instant into a blur of motion and purposefulness, and with its cocaine glow of unlimited, interlocked, immortal energy. Kurtz loved jazz and the blues.

After the last set, Pearl, Beau, and the pianist—a white kid named Coe Pierce—came over to join him for a drink before closing. Kurtz had known Beau and Pearl years ago. He wanted to buy them a drink, but he barely had enough money to pay for his beer. They chatted about old music, new jobs, and old times— tactfully ignoring the past decade or so of Kurtz's absence, since even the piano kid seemed cued in on that—and eventually Blue Franklin's owner, Daddy Bruce Woles, a hearty, heavyset man so black that his skin glowed almost eggplant in the smoke-hazy spotlights, came over to join them. Kurtz had never seen Woles without the stub of a cigar in his mouth, and had never seen the cigar lighted.

"Joe, you got an admirer," said Daddy Bruce. He waved over more drinks for everyone, on the house.

Kurtz sipped his fresh beer and waited.

"Little runty guy in a grubby raincoat came in here three nights ago and again last night. Didn't pay any attention to the music. First time, Ruby was tending bar, and this dwarf lugs this big, like legal briefcase over and props it on the bar, asks about you. Ruby, she knows you're out, of course, and doesn't say anything. Says she never heard of you. The dwarf leaves. Ruby tells me. Last night, same dwarf in a dirty raincoat, same battered briefcase, only *I'm* at the bar. I never heard of you, either. I tried to get the dwarf's name, but he just left his beer and went out. Haven't seen him tonight. Friend of yours?"

Kurtz shrugged. "Does he look something like Danny DeVito?"

"Yeah," said Daddy Bruce. "Only not cute and cuddly like that, you know? Just turd-ugly all the way down."

"Someone told me that Sammy Levine's brother Manny's looking for me," said Kurtz. "Probably him."

"Oh, God," said Pearl. "Sammy Levine was a mean little dwarf, too."

"Used to use wood blocks on the pedals to drive that damn giant Pontiac he and Eddie Falco bombed around in," said Big Beau. Then, "Sorry, Joe, didn't mean to bring up sad times."

"That's okay," said Kurtz. "Anything sad, I got out of my system a long time ago."

"Doesn't sound like this Manny Levine dwarf has," said Daddy Bruce.

Kurtz nodded.

Pearl took his hand. "It seems like just yesterday that you and Sam were in here every night, all of us catching a late dinner and drinks after the last set, and then Sam not drinking because . . ."

"Because she was pregnant," finished Kurtz. "Yeah. Only I guess it seems like a while ago to me."

The vocalist and the tenor sax player glanced at each other and nodded.

"Rachel?" Beau said.

"With Sam's ex-husband," said Kurtz.

"She must be . . . what—eleven, twelve now?"

"Almost fourteen," said Kurtz.

"To good times again," said Pearl in that wonderful smoke-and-whiskey voice of hers. She lifted her glass.

They all lifted their glasses.

It was getting cold at night. As Kurtz walked back through alleys and parking lots to his warehouse, wearing the corduroy trousers and denim shirt Sophia Farino had given him—the shirt worn untucked to conceal the little .38 in his waistband—he briefly considered heading back to the office to sleep. At least the basement of the porno shop was heated. But he decided not to. What was the old maxim? Don't shit where you eat? Something like that. He wanted to keep business and business separate.

He was taking a shortcut down a long alley between warehouses, less than six blocks from his own warehouse, when a car pulled in at the end of the alley behind him. Headlights threw his shadow ahead of him on the potholed lane.

Kurtz glanced around. No doorways deep enough to hide in. A loading dock, but solid concrete—he could roll up onto it if the car accelerated toward him, but he could not slip under it. No fire escapes. Too far to run to the next street if the car came at him.

Not looking back, staggering slightly as if drunk, Kurtz pulled the .38 from his belt and palmed it.

The car moved slowly down the long alley behind him. From the sound of the V-8 engine, the thing was big—at least a Lincoln Town Car, possibly a real limo—and it was in no hurry. It stopped about fifty feet behind him.

Kurtz stepped into the corner where the loading dock met brick wall and let the pistol drop into his fingers. He cocked the hammer.

It was a limo. The headlights went out and in the dimmer glow of the parking lights, Kurtz could see the huge mass of the black car silhouetted against distant streetlights, its exhaust swirling around it like fog. A big man got out of the front passenger side and another big man stepped out of the rear left door. Both men reached under their blazer jackets to touch guns.

Kurtz set the hammer back in place, slid the small pistol back up into his palm, and walked toward the limousine. Neither of the bodyguards drew weapons or moved to frisk him.

Kurtz walked past the man holding the rear door open, glanced into the rear seat—illuminated by several halogen spots—and got into the car.

"Mr. Kurtz," said the old man seated there. He was wearing a tuxedo and had a Stewart-plaid lap robe over his legs.

Kurtz dropped into the jump seat opposite him. "Mr. Farino." He uncocked the pistol and slipped it back in his waistband.

The bodyguards closed the doors and remained outside in the cold.

CHAPTER 21

"How is your investigation proceeding, Mr. Kurtz?"

Kurtz made a rude noise. "Some investigation. I interviewed your former accountant's wife for about five minutes and she ended up dead within the hour. That's all I've done."

"Investigating was never your real purpose, Mr. Kurtz."

"Tell me about it. It was my idea, remember? And my real purpose seems to be working fine. They've made the first move on me."

"You don't mean Carl?"

"No," said Kurtz, "I mean whoever called the cops and set me up after they murdered—butchered—Mrs. Richardson. They'd arranged a yard-shank job on me as soon as I got in general population."

Don Farino rubbed his cheek. It was a particularly rosy cheek for such a sick old man. Kurtz wondered idly if the don used makeup.

"And have you determined who set you up for this?" asked Farino.

"It's been suggested that it was a mook named Malcolm Kibunte who sometimes works for your lawyer, Miles. Do you know this Kibunte or the knife-man he hangs with? Cutter?"

Farino shook his head. "One is not able to keep track of all the black trash that comes through town these days. I presume these two are black."

"Malcolm is," said Kurtz. "Cutter's described as albino-like."

"And who told you about the shank job and suggested these names to you, Mr. Kurtz?" Farino's eyes were rapt.

"Your daughter."

Farino blinked. "My daughter? You've spoken to Sophia?"

"I've more than spoken to her," said Kurtz. "She bailed me out of jail before I went to County, and then took me home with her and tried to fuck me to death."

Don Farino's thin lips pulled back from his teeth and his fingers clenched on his knees under the robe. "Be careful, Mr. Kurtz. You speak too candidly."

Kurtz shrugged. "You're paying me for the facts. That was the setup we agreed to through Little Skag before I got out—I'd be point man and Judas goat for you and flush out whoever's betraying you. It was your daughter who acted—both in the bailing and fucking departments—I'm just reporting."

"Sophia has always been strong-willed and . . . of questionable judgment in her sexual choices," said Farino.

Kurtz shrugged again. He didn't give a damn about the fact or the insult behind it.

"Sophia told you about the connection between Miles and these two killers?" Farino said softly. "Suggesting that she believes Miles is behind everything?"

"Yep. But that doesn't mean she's telling the truth. She could be running both Miles and Malcolm and his knife-freak buddy."

"But you said that she was the one who bailed you out and warned you about the yard contract on you, Mr. Kurtz."

"She bailed me out. I have to take her word for the yard shank at County."

"And why would she go to all that trouble and lie?" asked Farino.

"To check me out," suggested Kurtz. "To find out what I'm really up to and how much I know. To put herself above suspicion." Kurtz looked out the tinted windows. The alley was very dark. "Mr. Farino, Sophia met bail, took me home, and almost threw me into the sack. Maybe she's just a tramp, like you say, but I don't believe it was my magnetic personality that made her go out of her way to seduce me."

"I doubt that you required much seducing, Mr. Kurtz."

"That's not the point," said Kurtz. "The point is that you know how intelligent she is—hell, that's why you're afraid she might be behind Richardson's disappearance and the truck hijackings—so you see why it makes more sense that there's a motive behind her actions."

"But Sophia is in line to inherit my wealth and much of the legitimate family business," said the don, looking at his clenched hands.

"That's what she said," said Kurtz. "Do you know any reasons why she would want to hurry the process along?"

Don Farino turned his face away. "Sophia has always been . . . impatient. And she would like to be Don."

Kurtz laughed. "Women can't be dons."

"Perhaps Sophia does not accept that," said Farino with a thin smile.

"You're not quite as busy circling the drain or as out of the loop as everyone thinks, are you?" said Kurtz.

Farino looked back at Kurtz, and there was something almost demonic in the old man's gaze. "No, Mr. Kurtz. I am paralyzed from the waist down and temporarily—how did you put it? Out of the loop. But I am nowhere near circling the drain. And I have no intention of staying out of the loop."

Kurtz nodded. "Maybe your daughter just doesn't want to wait around like Prince Charles for five or six decades and is ready to help the succession along a little bit. What's the fancy name for whacking the Old Man—patricide?"

"You are a crude man, Mr. Kurtz." Farino smiled again. "But there has been no discussion of whacking to this point. I hired you to find out what is going on

with Richardson's disappearance and the truck hijackings."

Kurtz shook his head. "You hired me to be a target
so you could find out who the shooter is so as to pro-
tect your own ass, Farino. Why did you kill Carl?"

"Pardon me?"

"You heard me. Sophia said Carl 'died of complications.' Why did you put a hit on him?"

"Carl was a fool, Mr. Kurtz."

"No argument there, but why whack him? Why not
just cut him loose?"

"He knew too much about the family."

"Bullshit," said Kurtz. "The average cub reporter at
the *Buffalo Evening News* knows more about the work-
ings of your mob family than dear, departed, dipshit
Carl could've ever figured out. Why did you have him
whacked?"

Farino was silent for several moments. Kurtz listened to the heavy engine idle. One of the bodyguards
lit a cigarette, and the match flare was a small circle
of diffused light in the black alley.

"I wanted to put her in touch with a certain . . . technician," Farino said at last.

"A hit man," said Kurtz. "Someone from outside the
family."

"Yes."

"Someone outside the Mafia?"

Farino showed an expression of distaste, as if Kurtz
had farted in his expensive limousine. "Someone from
outside the organizational structure, yes."

Kurtz chuckled. "You sonofabitch. You wanted Sophia to spend time with this hit man just to see if she'd

hire him to kill me. Ol' Carl died just so you'd have a reason for this operator and your little girl to chat."

Farino said nothing.

"Did she?" said Kurtz. "Hire him to kill me?"

"No."

"What's this technician's name?"

"Since he was not hired, his name is of no concern."

"It is to me," said Kurtz, and there was an undertone to his voice. "I want to know all the players." He touched the .38 in his belt.

Farino smiled, as if the idea of Kurtz's shooting him and getting away alive were amusing. Then the smile faded as the don considered the fact that Kurtz might do the former without worrying about the latter. "No one knows this man's name," he said.

Kurtz waited.

"He's known as the Dane," Farino said after another long silence.

"Holy shit," breathed Kurtz.

"You've heard of him?" Farino's smile was back.

"Who hasn't? The Kennedy mob connections in the seventies. Jimmy Hoffa. There are rumors that the Dane was behind that lovely underpass hit in Paris, where he used just the little car, no weapon."

"There are always rumors," agreed Farino. "Aren't you going to ask for a description of the Dane?"

It was Kurtz's turn to smile. "From what I hear, it wouldn't do a damn bit of good. This guy is supposed to be better at disguises than the Jackal at the height of his powers. The only good news is that if Sophia *had* hired him, I'd know it because I'd be dead already."

"Yes," said Farino. "So what is our next step, Mr. Kurtz?"

"Well, tonight's your truck delivery from the Vancouver source. If it's hit, we'll go from there. I'll make myself obvious in investigating it. If Kibunte is involved—whoever's involved—it makes sense for them to come after me next."

"Good luck, Mr. Kurtz."

Kurtz opened the door and the bodyguard held it for him. "Why wish me that?" Kurtz said to Farino. "Whether I have luck or not, you get the information you need. And if I'm dead, you keep the fifty thousand we agreed to."

"Quite true," said the don. "But I may have a future use for you, and the fifty thousand is a small amount to pay for peace of mind."

"I wouldn't know," said Kurtz and stepped out into the alley.

CHAPTER 22

Old mob guys who never quite became made men don't die, they just end up as truck drivers for the mob.

Charlie Scruggs and Oliver Battaglia had both been low-level button men back during the Genovese era, but now, in their golden retirement years, were driving this goddamn truck all the way from Vancouver to Buffalo. Charlie was sixty-nine years old and stout and leathery, with a face full of burst blood vessels; he still wore his Teamsters cap everywhere and proudly told everyone of the week he spent as personal driver and bodyguard to Jimmy Hoffa. He had the constitution of a healthy pit bull. Oliver was tall, thin, saturnine, a chain-smoker, only sixty-two but sick much of the time, and—Charlie Scruggs now knew after eight of these damned Vancouver-Buffalo runs—an absolute pain in the ass.

The truck was no eighteen-wheeler, just a basic six-
ton carryall: what Charlie had called a deuce-and-a-
half back in Korea. Because it was a smaller truck, it
could go on backroads and even on streets without
much notice. Charlie did all the driving; Oliver rode
shotgun—literally, since there was a sawed-off shotgun in the concealed compartment at the top rear of
the cab—but Oliver was so slow that Charlie put his
faith in the Colt .45 semiautomatic that he kept in a
quick-draw holster under his seat.

In eighteen years of driving trucks for the Organization, neither Charlie nor Oliver had ever had to draw
his weapons. That was the benefit of working for the
Organization.

The drawback was that they had to take the goddamned long way to Buffalo. Not only driving two-
thirds the way across Canada—a country Charlie hated
with a passion—but not even taking the direct route
down through Michigan, back into Canada at Detroit,
and up along the north side of Lake Erie. The problem
was Customs. More specifically, the problem was that
the Canadian and American Customs guys on the arm
for the Farino family worked only the night shift at the
same time a certain Thursday of the month at the same
place: the Queenston Toll Bridge at Lewiston, about
six miles north of the Falls. They were getting close.
After more than seventy-two hours on the road, Charlie
was creeping the truck north out of the Canadian city
of Niagara Falls, on the scenic road that ran along the
river and gorge. Of course, it wasn't very scenic now—
a little after 2:00 A.M.—and neither Charlie nor Oliver
would have given a shit about the view in the daylight,

but Charlie had orders to stay off the QEW that ran
along the shore of Lake Ontario—too many eager
Mounties—so he'd had to take Highway 20 down from
Hamilton and then head north again from the Falls.

The truck was filled with stolen VCRs and DVD
players. Even crammed full, the deuce-and-a-half
couldn't hold all that many machines, so Charlie wondered where the profit was. He knew, of course, that
the decks were being dumped after being used to copy
pirate tapes and discs, but it was still a mystery why
the Organization thought it was worth their while to
ship a few score of the units all the way from Vancouver to a has-been family in Buffalo.

Ah, well, thought Charlie, *ours is not to wonder why,
ours is but to do and die.*

A few miles below the big park at Canada's Queenston Heights, Charlie pulled the truck into an empty
rest area. He shook Oliver awake. "Watch the truck. I
gotta go take a piss."

Oliver grunted but rubbed his eyes. Charlie shook
his head, went into the empty visitors' center perched
right on the edge of the Niagara Gorge just north of
the whirlpool, and took his piss. When he came out
and crawled back up into the cab, Oliver was sleeping
again with his bony chin on his bony chest.

"Goddamn you," said Charlie and shook the shotgun
man.

Oliver went face forward into the metal dash. Blood
trickled out of his left ear.

Charlie stared for a fatal minute and then went for
his .45. Too late. Both doors were flung open and an

array of grinning black faces and aimed pistol muzzles pointed his way.

"Hey, Charles, my man," said the tallest jig, who had a goddamned diamond in his front tooth and was waving a huge gun. "It's cool, my man. Forget the piece, Charles." The jig held up Charlie's pistol and then dropped it back in his jacket pocket. He pointed the huge revolver. "Just be cool a minute, and then you be on your way again."

Charlie Scruggs had had guns pointed at him before, and was still around to tell about it. He didn't like the fact that they knew his name, but Oliver may have told them that. He was not about to be intimidated by this pissant. "Nigger," he said, "you have no idea the shit you just stepped in. Do you know who this truck belongs to?"

Several of the blacks, especially the one near Oliver wearing a red do-rag, began glowering hate/kill looks, but the tall bald black just looked surprised. "Who it belong to, Charles?" he said, his eyes widening like Stepin Fetchit's.

"The Farino Family," said Charlie Scruggs.

The black's eyes got wider. "Oh, my goodness gracious, heavens to Betsy," he said in a fag voice. "Do you mean the *Mafia* Farino family?"

"I mean this truck and everything in it—including Oliver and me—are Organization property you coon sonofabitch," said Charlie. "You touch anything in it, and there won't be a shithole in Central America where you can hide your black ass."

The bald man nodded thoughtfully. "You probably right, Charles, my man. But I guess it be too late." He glanced mournfully at Oliver. "We done already touch Ollie there."

Charlie glanced at his dead companion and tried to phrase his next sentence carefully.

The jig did not give him the chance to speak. "Plus, Charlie, my man, you already use the N-word."

Malcolm shot Charlie Scruggs through the left eye.

"Hey!" screamed Doo-Rag from the opposite side, ducking low behind Oliver's body. "Tell me when you about to do that, motherfucker."

"Shut the fuck up," said Malcolm. " 'Jectory be *up*. See Charles's brains on the roof there? You in no danger, nigger."

Doo-Rag glowered.

"Get the machines," said Malcolm.

Doo-Rag flashed a last look but went around behind the truck, cut the padlock with bolt cutters, and crawled in. A couple of minutes later he came around the driver's side carrying a stack of DVD players.

"You sure they the right ones?" said Malcolm.

"Yeah, I sure I'm sure," said Doo-Rag. He pointed to the decal with the serial number on top of each of the players.

Malcolm nodded and Cutter came around the front of the truck. The others made way for him. Cutter removed a small knife from his pocket, pulled open a screwdriver blade, and opened the back of the top DVD.

"You right for a change, Doo." Malcolm nodded again, Cutter took the DVD players, and everyone except for Doo-Rag and Malcolm headed for the Astro Van. "Start the engine," said Malcolm. "Set the block."

"Fuck that," said Doo-Rag. "All that blood and brains and shit. Top of the fucker's head *gone,* man. Dude could be HIV positive or something."

Malcolm grinned and set the barrel of his huge Smith & Wesson Model 686 Powerport .357 Magnum up alongside Doo-Rag's head. "Get the keys. Start the truck. Set the block."

Doo-Rag crawled in and did all those things. The engine roared as the wooden block was jammed against the accelerator.

"Now," said Malcolm, stepping back, "trick be to pop that brake off, put it in gear, and get the fuck off the running board before truck get *there,* my man." Malcolm pointed to the edge of the gorge less than fifty feet in front of the truck. There was a light fence there, but no guardrails. Some traffic passed on the road, but no cars pulled into the empty rest area.

Doo-Rag smirked, kicked the brake off, leaned delicately over Charlie's slumped, bleeding corpse, kicked in the clutch, and hit the gearshift lever.

The truck bounced over the concrete parking chock and tore up frozen turf as it roared for the fence.

Doo-Rag rode along for a minute, swinging on the running board, stepping off nonchalantly at the last possible second before the truck tore through the fence and plummeted out of sight, ripping trees and branches off the side of the cliff as it went.

Malcolm set the .357 back in its long shoulder holster under his topcoat and applauded. Doo-Rag ignored him and watched the truck fall.

It was a little over two hundred feet to the river below. This gave the truck time to do a half gainer,

Charlie's corpse flying out the open door in the dark, before the vehicle slammed, upside down, into the huge rocks right at the edge of the swirling water. Dozens of VCRs and DVD players went flying out over the river, each one making its own splash. One of them almost made it as far upriver as the whirlpool. Everyone in the van cheered at the noise that came up out of the deep gorge.

There was no explosion. No fire.

Charlie had been planning to gas up on the American side, where the fuel was cheaper.

CHAPTER 23

"I didn't really expect to see you again, Mr. Kurtz," said Peg O'Toole.

"The feeling was mutual," said Kurtz. He had left the office phone as his contact number, and Parole Officer Peg O'Toole had called saying that he was required to come in to finish his first appointment. Arlene had said that O'Toole had sounded a bit surprised that Kurtz had a real, live secretary.

"Shall we pick up where we left off?" said O'Toole. "We were discussing the fact that you needed a permanent address within the next week or so."

"Sure," said Kurtz, "but can I ask a question?"

The parole officer removed her tortoiseshell glasses and waited. Her eyes were green and cool.

"When they dragged me out of here," said Kurtz, "they wanted to pin a murder rap on me when they knew I wasn't involved. During the arraignment, the charge was changed to illegal possession of a firearm and violating parole. Now that's been dropped."

"What is your question, Mr. Kurtz?"

"I'd like to know what you had to do with the charge being dropped."

O'Toole tapped her lower lip with the stem of her glasses. "Why do you think I had something to do with the charges being dropped?"

"Because I think Hathaway . . . the homicide cop who dragged me out of here . . ."

"I know Detective Hathaway," said O'Toole. There was the slightest hint of revulsion in her tone.

". . . I think he would have gone ahead with the illegal-carry parole-violation charge," finished Kurtz. "During the interrogation at the city jail, he showed me a throwdown he was ready to plant on me, and I know that he wants me in County for his own reasons."

"I don't know about any of that," O'Toole said curtly. "But I did check into your arraignment"—she hesitated a few seconds—"and I did let the district attorney know that I was present during your arrest and watched the detectives frisk you. You weren't armed when they arrested you."

"You told the D.A. *that*?" said Kurtz, amazed. When O'Toole said nothing more, he said, "What if Hathaway testified that I had an ankle holster or something?"

"I watched them frisk you," she said coolly. "There was no ankle holster."

Kurtz shook his head, truly surprised. He had never heard of a cop going out of his or her way to keep another cop from railroading someone.

"Can we get back to your interview?" she asked.

"Sure."

"Someone answered the phone number you gave me and identified herself as your secretary . . ."

"Arlene," said Kurtz.

". . . but anyone can claim to be anyone on the phone," finished O'Toole. "I'd like to visit your business office. Did I say something amusing, Mr. Kurtz?"

"Not at all, Officer O'Toole." He gave her the address. "If you call ahead, Arlene will let you in the back way. It might be preferable to coming in the front."

"And why is that?" Her tone was suspicious.

Kurtz told her.

This time it was the P.O. who smiled. "I worked Vice for three years, Mr. Kurtz. I can probably take a transit through a porno shop."

Kurtz was surprised for the second time. He didn't know of many parole officers who had been real cops.

"I saw you on the *Channel Seven WKBW Eyewitness News* yesterday evening," she said and waited.

Kurtz also waited.

"Is there any special reason," she said at last, "that you happened to be at the site where a truck had gone into the gorge the night before?"

"Just rubbernecking," said Kurtz. "I was driving along the expressway up there, saw the TV trucks, and pulled into the turnout to see what all the commotion was."

O'Toole made a note on her pad. "Were you on the American side or the Canadian side?" Her tone was casual.

Kurtz actually grinned. "If it had been the Canadian side, Parole Officer O'Toole, I would have been in violation of my parole, and you'd be sending me to County within the hour. No, I think you could tell from the angle that they were shooting video from the American side. I guess they couldn't get a clear shot from where the truck actually went over."

O'Toole made another note. "You seemed almost eager to be seen in the cutaway shots to the crowd," she said.

Kurtz shrugged. "Isn't everyone eager to get on TV?"

"I don't think you are, Mr. Kurtz. At least, not unless you had a specific reason to be seen there."

Kurtz looked blandly at her and thought, *Christ, I'm glad Hathaway isn't as smart as she is.*

She checked something else off her list. "All right, about your place of residence. Are you settled yet?"

"Not really," said Kurtz, "but I'm getting closer to finding a permanent place to live."

"What are your plans?"

"Eventually," said Kurtz, "I'd like one of those big houses on the bluffs up toward Youngstown, not far from Fort Niagara."

O'Toole glanced at her watch and waited.

"In the immediate future," said Kurtz, "I'm hoping to find an apartment."

"Week after next," said O'Toole, putting down her pen and removing her glasses to let him know that the interview was over. "That's when I'll make the official visit."

CHAPTER 24

The Alabama Beagle Boys—back when there were five of them, there were only four living now—came by their name via an unfortunate photograph picked up by the wire services in the mid-1990s when an Alabama Department of Corrections official, exhilarated by his popular press after bringing back chain gangs, issued horizontally striped prison uniforms to all state inmates. The photographer from the Dothan, Alabama, newspaper had gone out to one of the prison-striped chain gangs working along State Highway 84 not far from the Boll Weevil Monument and photographed five men pulled from the work detail apparently at random.

It had not been random. It had amused the gang bull to line up five dim-witted brothers for the shot, the five overweight young men all serving three years for a completely botched Wal-Mart robbery in Dothan during which thirty-five legally armed Wal-Mart shoppers—the majority of them senior citizens—and the seventy-four-year-old "Wal-Mart Greeter," who had been carrying a .357 Magnum, all had drawn down on the boys, putting four of them in the hospital for gunshot wounds and sending all of them to the Babbie State Prison just outside of Opp. The five were known then just as the Beugel brothers—Warren, Darren, Douglas, Andrew, and Oliver—but a combination of a *Dothan Journal* misprint that went out to UPI and the comic image of the five in their striped coveralls changed their name forever to the Alabama Beagle Boys.

Six months after the photograph was taken, four of them escaped—Oliver, the youngest, had crawled back through the wire to rescue his pet crayfish and had been shot twenty-four times by guards. The first thing the Beagle Boys did after eluding the "Largest Manhunt in Southern Alabama History" was to visit the Department of Corrections' Chief's farm outside of Montgomery, where they killed the man, burned down his house, raped his wife into a coma, and nailed the family's dog to the barn door (although those still in prison in the South maintain that it was the dog who was raped and the wife who was nailed to the barn door).

Warren, Darren, Douglas, and Andrew then headed for Canada but, stymied by the difficulty of crossing the border under the delusion that they needed passports, went to ground in Buffalo, where they became lay ministers and soldiers in the White Aryan Army of the Lord, headquartered in the suburb of West Seneca.

This night, at a warehouse near the State University of New York campus, they were shopping.

"Full auto with laser shit is what we want," said Warren, the oldest.

"Of course, of course," said Malcolm Kibunte, bowing the huge rednecks into the rear room of the cinderblock warehouse. "Full auto with laser shit it will be, then."

The Boys had been carefully and repeatedly frisked before being driven, blindfolded, to the warehouse site, where Doo-Rag and a dozen of his men watched carefully and a bit reproachfully. The Alabama Beagle Boys ignored the gangbangers.

"Holy shit," breathed Douglas, who, after Oliver, had always been the least brilliant of the five, "lookit here. Woowhee! Everythang we wanted, rat heah."

"Shut up, Douglas," Andrew said automatically.

Douglas was right, however. The long warehouse room was stacked with boxes of weapons and ammo. Laid out for inspection were AR-15s, M590A1 Pistol Grip mil-spec combat shotguns, Colt M4 full-auto carbines, combat-ready M-16s, compact machine guns such as HK UMP 45s and Israeli Bullpups, and sniper rifles such as Remington's model 700 Police DM Light Tactical.

All four of the Boys wanted to drool. Three of them resisted the impulse, but their small eyes were all alight. If the Boys saw any irony in buying weapons for the coming Race War Heralding Armageddon from black gang members, they did not show it. Of course, the Boys were not deeply into irony.

Darren was ogling a table filled with detachable sights: Aimpoint Red Dots, Bausch & Lomb 10 × 42 Police Tactical Scopes, U.S. Optics SN4 SpecOps Battle Sights, Comp ML red dots, and others.

"Careful, Darren, my man," said Malcolm. "Your hard-on showing. Weaken your bargaining position, you cum on the hardware." Malcolm grinned broadly to show that it was all good humor between guys.

Darren blushed and turned his back.

Warren was mixing and matching elements into a perfect weapon: the Colt M4 carbine with a compact laser sight, topped off with a Suppressed Tactical Weapons suppressor made out of gold-colored titanium.

"Good choice," said Malcolm. "A handsome combination to take to Armageddon, that be God's truth."

Warren glared but said only, "How much?"

"For how many of which?" said Malcolm.

The Boys licked their lips, looking around in a palpable heat wave of greed, while Warren took a wrinkled sheet of yellow legal-pad paper from his hip pocket—the Boys were all wearing old army fatigue jackets, jump boots, and jeans now rather than their trademark stripes—and consulted his shopping list. He read from the list slowly, obviously adding a few things from the displays.

Malcolm raised his eyebrows and named a price.

The Boys looked at each other in near despair. With the money the White Aryan Army of the Lord had raised so far, they could not quite afford Warren's single carbine-scope-suppressor combination.

"Let us go outsad an' fahr a few of these-here guns," Andrew said craftily.

Malcolm just grinned while Doo-Rag clicked his Tek-9 to full-auto. "Not quite time for test fahring yet, my man," said Malcolm.

"Maybe it'd be time for the police to hear that some Buffalo niggers were the ones who knocked over the Dunkirk army arsenal this past August," said Warren.

"Maybe," Malcolm agreed with a grin. "But if there come even a rumor like that—and we'd hear it because the *po*-lice wouldn't know where to find these niggers or their guns—then the poor old Chapel of the Good Ol' Boy Aryan Nation Crackers for Jesus gets itself visited by fifty-sixty of Doo-Rag's friends, and the Aryan Nation faithful get themselves shot into little greasy mini-Aryan chickenbits."

"White Aryan Army of the Lord," corrected Douglas.

"Shut up, Douglas," said Andrew.

There were a few moments of silence.

"There *is* a way that you can get a thirty percent discount on some of the things you want here," Malcolm said at last.

"How?" said Warren.

Malcolm wandered over, picked up a Carbon AR-15 .223, sighted through the Colt C-More red-dot sight, dry-fired the black weapon, and set it back. "There a dude that's going to die," he said. "He hiding out in a warehouse in the city. Not armed with nothing more than a pistol. Maybe not that. You take care of it for us, thirty percent off on whatever you carry in to do the job."

Warren squinted at Malcolm. "That don't make no sense." He looked around at the boxes upon boxes of weapons and then at Doo-Rag and his heavily armed friends.

Malcolm shrugged. "This dude a white boy. You know how sensitive we are these days about offing white boys."

"Bull*shit*," said Andrew.

"Shut up, Andrew," said Warren. To Malcolm, he said, "You want this guy wasted, why don't you just take him out on the street with one of those?" He nodded toward one of the scoped sniper rifles on display.

Malcolm made a gesture with his hands. "Agreed, be easy to do," he said. "But sometimes the Buffalo police take notice when you gun down citizens on their streets—you understand what I'm saying? Better let this white boy die and rot away in this old abandoned warehouse."

"Then why don't you go in after him yourselves?" said Warren.

Malcolm shrugged. "Doo-Rag and the others want to, but there always a chance that something might go wrong—we drop a weapon or something—and then the federal 'thorities got an idea who borrowed their army toys."

Warren grinned, showing southern Alabama's Department of Corrections' lack of investment in dental care. "But if we leave prints behind . . . or one of us left behind . . . it don't bother you-all."

"Not so much," Malcolm agreed.

"When do you want this done?" Darren asked.

"Real soon would be fine," said Malcolm. "You choose the pieces you want with the toys to go with them, we take you to where this dude is sleeping. Thirty percent off, you each get a piece for the price of that one you wanted. Plus all the laser shit you want. Plus some other good stuff . . ." Malcolm held up a heavy double-optic apparatus with nylon straps.

"What the *shit* is that?" said Darren.

"Shut up, Darren," said Warren. "What the shit *is* it?" he asked Malcolm.

Malcolm raised an eyebrow. "Ain't you never seen one of those movies where the terrorists or Navy SEALS or such wear this night-vision shit?"

"Oh, yeah," said Darren. "They just look different when they're not on someone's head is all."

"Shut up, Darren," said Warren. "Night-vision goggles?" he said to Malcolm.

"Correct, my man," said Malcolm. "These take the tiniest little bit of light—not even to notice, dark as a cave to the naked eyeball—and let you see like it was high noon. These goggles here probably led to a shitload of Iraqis going to Allah early."

Douglas whistled.

"Shut up, Douglas," Andrew said automatically.

"You said do this real soon," said Warren. "How soon is real soon?"

Malcolm checked his watch. It was almost 1:00 A.M. "Now be good," he said.

"And we just get to walk away from this place with the guns?" Warren asked.

Malcolm nodded.

"And you gonna give us bullets?" Darren asked.

Warren glared at his brother, but said nothing.

"Yes, Darren, my man, bullets thrown in for free before you go into the warehouse. We got clips of .223s, .45s, subsonic 5.56 millimeters for the Bullpup, .22s, 9 millimeters for some of the carbines, banana clips, 12-gauge shells for the shotguns, even some .308 Match for the sniper shit."

Malcolm lifted some brightly colored hand radios, gesturing like a salesman ready to close a deal. "And we even throw in these personal, multi-frequency portable radios with a two-mile range for free."

"Shit," said Darren. "Those are just kiddie toys."

Malcolm smiled and shrugged. "True, my man. But you understand why once we drop you off—with *ammo* clips and Kevlar vests as well as the guns—we don't want to wait around."

Warren screwed up his face, thinking about this. His silence suggested that he could find no fault in the logic.

"You can use the radios to talk to each other going in," said Malcolm. "Then call us when it all over."

Warren grunted. "How do we know when it's the right dude?"

Malcolm grinned. "Well, since this white boy the only person in the warehouse, just kill everybody in there, you probably be safe to assume," he said. "But this might help." He tossed Kurtz's mug shot onto the table covered with laser sights and night-vision goggles.

The Alabama Beagle Boys huddled around the table, staring down at the photograph, none of them touching it.

"Shall we do it?" said Malcolm, gesturing to the displays of weapons.

"We didn't bring cash," said Warren.

Malcolm smiled. "Your credit good with us. Besides, we know where your church is."

CHAPTER 25

The stupid shits came in the front door and now they're using the elevator. Probably trying to flush me—scare me into running downstairs.

Kurtz did not know who the stupid shits were, but he had rigged the front and rear doors of the warehouse with monofilament thread that ran up to his sixth-floor sleeping cubby, each thread ending in a soup can full of rocks, and his front-door can had rattled. Kurtz had been out of his sleeping bag in two seconds, had slipped into his shoes and leather gloves, had pulled his .45 and the short-barreled .38 from his duffel, and was out into the pitch-black hallway in ten seconds, crouching and waiting. The terrible noise of the freight elevator spoke for itself.

Kurtz had no night-vision goggles, but his eyes had long since adapted to the tiny bit of cloud-reflected city light filtering down through holes in the ceiling and down the elevator shaft itself. Moving carefully around heaps of junk and puddles of water, he moved quickly to the open elevator shaft.

Usually, he knew, elevator doors were designed not to open if the elevator was not stopped on that level, but the construction boys had ripped off the wide doors to the freight elevator for reasons known only to God and themselves, marking the elevator shaft with only a ribbon of orange plastic tape stretched across the dark opening. Kurtz crouched by the tape and waited. *The elevator could be a diversion. They could be coming up the stairways.* From where he crouched, Kurtz could see the opening to the north stairwell.

Someone was talking in loud whispers in the elevator.

As the top of the freight elevator reached the level of his floor, Kurtz stepped out onto its roof and went to one knee, a pistol in each hand. He made no noise, but the grinding and growl of cables and the ancient motor would have shielded the sound of his move even if he had been wearing metal boots.

The elevator did not stop on his floor, but ground its way up to the top floor, seven. The huge elevator door cranked open and three men inside stepped out, still whispering to one another.

Kurtz had ridden on the elevator roof before and knew there was a hole in the plaster through which he could look out onto the seventh-floor mezzanine. He knew where it was because he had made the hole himself some days ago, using a crowbar to tear through the plaster. To his right was a piece of cardboard nailed

over another hole he had made, this one in the west
wall of the elevator shaft; he knew from practice that
he could crawl out that hole and roll onto some reposi-
tioned construction scaffolding in five seconds.

The seventh floor received more light than the lower
six floors: as dirty as the ancient skylight above was,
it still allowed some starlight and city light in. The
walls here had been removed to make this a
mezzanine-apartment level. The interior opening to the
atrium seven floors below was sealed off only by sta-
pled floor-to-ceiling construction plastic. Kurtz could
easily see the three men, even while it was obvious
that they were having problems seeing anything.

What the hell? thought Kurtz. He had expected Malcolm and his men. He had no idea who these clumsy-
looking white idiots were. Kurtz knew at once that
these weren't Don Farino's bodyguards: the old don
would never hire help with such bad haircuts and six-
day beards. And, despite their arsenal, they didn't look
like cops.

The three men were all large and overweight, their
bulk increased by what looked to be Kevlar vests under
army jackets. They were heavily armed with automatic
weapons, all three of which were sighted with pro-
jecting lasers, the beams quite visible in the dripping
water and floating plaster dust. All three men were
wearing bulky night-vision goggles.

A radio squawked. The tallest of the three answered
it while the other two kept sweeping the mezzanine
with their laser beams. Within seconds, Kurtz had to
wonder whether he was being attacked by the Confed-
erate Army.

"Warren?"

"Yeah, Andrew, what is it? I told you not to radio unless it was important." *Ah tole you nat to radio 'less it was imporant.*

"You all okay up there, Warren?" *Y'all okay . . .*

"Goddamn it, Andrew, we just got here. Now shut the hell up unless we call you or unless you see him. We're going to chase him your way."

Kurtz slid his .45 into his back holster and took the heavy sap out of his pocket.

The tallest of the three men clicked off the hand radio and gestured for the other two to split up, one going around the west mezzanine and the other around the east side. Kurtz watched them go, the big men moving in what looked like a parody of military efficiency, stumbling over heaps of construction debris, cursing when they stepped in puddles, all the time fiddling with their night-vision apparatuses.

Warren stayed behind, head moving, aiming a Colt M4 carbine burdened with a huge suppressor. The big man swiveled constantly, the laser beam flickering left, right, up, down. Warren glanced behind him, made sure that no one was between him and the wall near the elevator, and backed up cautiously.

The radio squawked again.

"What?" Warren said angrily.

"Nothing up here. Me and Douglas are at the stairway at the other end."

"You look in all the goddamn rooms?"

"Yeah. They ain't got doors on this level."

"Okay," said Warren. "Start on down. Sweep the sixth floor."

"You comin' down, Warren?"

"I'm staying right here until you got the sixth floor swept. We don't wanna be comin' at each other in the dark, now, do we?"

"No."

"So call me when you got the whole floor searched, then I'll come down, then you do the next one down, until we find the sonofabitch or flush him down to where Andrew is waiting. Y'all understand, Darren?"

"Yeah."

Another voice. "Darren, Douglas, Warren? Y'all all right?"

Three voices at once. "Shut up, Andrew."

While all this chatting was going on, Warren had been backing up until he was almost to the scaffolding. Kurtz silently lifted the cardboard panel and moved out of the elevator shaft.

The wooden plank creaked under him. Warren started to turn. Kurtz leaned forward and sapped him with the two-pound blackjack.

CHAPTER 26

Andrew didn't like being alone on the first floor. It was dark and dank and creepy down here. Looking through his night-vision goggles made everything go all greenish white, so that every doorway or heap of sand looked like a ghost. But when he took the goggles off—which Warren had told him not to do—he couldn't see anything at all. The Israeli Bullpup full-auto assault rifle that he'd chosen was cool, slick, and black and curved as a snake, but he couldn't really see it in the dark. At least it wasn't heavy. Even the laser-sight's red beam, which had seemed so cool at the niggers' warehouse, was just a greenish beam of light through his goggles. Andrew amused himself by playing *Star Wars* with it, making light-saber noises as he swung the Bullpup and swooshed the beam back and forth down the long hallway.

Suddenly the radio crackled again. It was Darren.

"Warren? Warren? We found this Kurtz's guy's hidey-hole on six! He ain't here, but we found a cot and sleeping bag and shit. Warren?"

Warren did not answer.

"Warren?" came Douglas's voice.

"Warren?" said Andrew from his place near the front hall on the first floor.

"Shut up, Andrew!" said Darren and Douglas together. Then, also together, they said, "Warren? Warren?"

Warren didn't answer.

"Y'all better get back up there," said Andrew.

This time his two older brothers did not tell him to shut up. There was a silence broken only by static-crackle and then Douglas said, "Yeah. You stay where you are, Andrew. If you see somethin' move, don't shoot until you're sure it ain't us comin' down. If it ain't us, kill it."

"Okay," said Andrew.

"An' stay the hell off the radio," said Darren.

"Okay," said Andrew. He could hear the clicks as they turned their radios off.

Andrew stood silent for what seemed a very long time. He was still turning slowly, trying to get used to the glowing greenish world of the night-vision goggles, but even the light-saber game wasn't any fun anymore. Nothing moved from the east stairwell. The elevator remained silent. Water dripped. Finally Andrew couldn't stand it any longer. He pressed the *transmit* button on the small sports walkie-talkie. "Warren?"

Silence.

"Douglas? Darren?"

No answer. Andrew repeated the call and then shut his own radio off. He was getting nervous.

It was lighter in the big middle part of the warehouse—the part that Warren had called the atrium—and Andrew moved into the huge, echoing space, looking up more than seven stories to the glowing skylight almost one hundred feet above him. It was only reflected city light bouncing off clouds coming through the skylight, but it flared up so much in Andrew's goggles that he was blinded for a second. He raised his free hand to wipe the tears from his eyes, but the stupid night-vision goggles were in the way.

Andrew looked up at the top floor, where floor-to-ceiling plastic reflected the light differently than did the cold brick of the first six floors, but nothing was visible through the thick plastic. He lifted the radio again.

"Warren, Douglas, Darren? Y'all all right?"

As if in answer there came seven shots—very rapid, very loud, not silenced at all—and suddenly a terrible ripping and screaming from high up near the skylight.

Andrew swung the Bullpup assault rifle up.

There was a hole in the plastic way up there on the seventh floor. Worse than that, something huge and loud was screaming and flapping its way down toward him. Through his goggles, the thing looked like some gigantic, misshapen, greenish white bat-thing with one blazing eye. Its wings must have been twenty feet long, and they were flapping wildly, now streaming behind the body of the bat like rippling ribbons of white fire. The bat was screeching as it fell toward him.

Andrew emptied the generous clip of the Bullpup at the apparition. He had time to see that the burning eye of the thing was actually the dot of his laser beam and also to see several of his slugs hit home, tearing into the spinning, flapping bat-thing, but the screaming continued—grew worse, if anything.

Andrew jumped back into the atrium doorway, but kept shooting—*phut! phut! phut! phut!*—he had never heard a silenced weapon on full-auto before and the ripping sound mixed with the screaming and flapping noises weirded him out.

The giant bat hit the concrete floor about thirty feet from Andrew. Now it sounded and looked more like a giant Hefty bag full of vegetable soup hitting the ground than any sort of bat that Andrew had ever seen. Green-white liquid spilled and spurted in every direction and it took only a few seconds for Andrew to realize that it was blood and that it would be quite red in real light.

Andrew ripped off his night-vision goggles, threw them down, and ran for the front door.

Kurtz had sapped the big man lightly: enough to knock him out, but not hard enough to kill him or keep him out for long. Kurtz jumped from the scaffold and worked quickly, moving the moaning man's Colt M4 carbine out of reach, patting him down for other weapons—he carried none—confiscating his radio and night-vision goggles, and finally pulling off his filthy army jacket and donning it himself. Kurtz was cold.

The radio crackled again. Kurtz listened to the one on the first floor talking to the two on the sixth floor who'd found his cot and sleeping bag.

"Y'all better get back up there," came the brain-damaged drawl from the cracker downstairs.

Kurtz heard either Darren or Douglas say, "Yeah" and then he got busy retrieving the Colt M4, checking that the magazine was full and the safety off, and then lying prone behind the moaning—but still unstirring—facedown figure of Warren. Kurtz did not prefer to use long guns, but he knew how to use them. Lying there, the barrel of the M4 propped on the big man's back, Kurtz felt like a figure in an old cowboy painting—the cavalryman who's had to shoot his horse to use as cover when the Indians are attacking.

If these particular Indians used the nearest stairway, they'd be coming up the north stairwell next to the elevators just ten yards away. If they came up the south stairwell, they could approach from either the east or west mezzanine, but Kurtz would hear them either way.

They came up the north stairwell and made enough noise to make the groaning Warren almost wake.

Kurtz sighed just before the two came into sight. If they paused at the doorway to the stairwell, he might be in trouble lying there behind Warren. But he did not think they would pause and come onto the seventh floor one at a time. Everything they'd done so far had been stupid or stupider. Kurtz sighed because he had no anger toward these idiots, even though they'd obviously come to kill him.

They exploded onto the landing, rifles seeking a target, laser beams whipping left and right, shouting at each other, both men obviously half-blinded by the glare of the ambient light in their goggles. Kurtz took a breath, sighted on the pale faces above the black Kevlar, and shot twice. He noticed how efficient the titanium silencer was on the M4. Both men went down heavily and did not rise again.

"Warren?" crackled the radio in Kurtz's army jacket pocket. "Douglas? Darren?"

Kurtz gave it another minute, made sure that the two men's rifles had fallen far from their hands, and then rose and moved quickly to the fallen figures. Both were dead. He dropped the M4 and walked quickly back to Warren, who was beginning to stir.

Kurtz set his boot on the big man's neck and jaw and forced the face back down against the concrete. Warren's eyes flickered open and Kurtz pressed the muzzle of the .45 pistol forcefully into his left eyesocket. "Don't move," he whispered.

Warren groaned but ceased trying to rise to his knees.

"Names," Kurtz whispered.

"Huh?"

Kurtz pressed harder with the pistol. "Do you know my name?"

"Kurtz." Warren's breath kicked up concrete dust.

"Who sent you?"

Warren's breathing slowed. Kurtz was certain that he had not been conscious during the shooting. The big man was obviously thinking things over now and trying to come up with a plan. Kurtz didn't want him to have that luxury. He thumbed the hammer back on the .45 with an audible click and pressed the muzzle deeper into Warren's eye socket. "Who sent you?"

"Nigger. . . ." said Warren.

Kurtz pressed harder. "Names."

Warren tried to shake his head, but the pressure from Kurtz's boot and pistol made that impossible. "Don't know his name. Guy who runs drugs to the Bloods. Has a diamond in his tooth."

"Where?" said Kurtz. "How'd you contact him? Where do I find him?"

Warren blew concrete dust. "Seneca Social Club. Nigger place. Sent Darren out to make contact. They have a warehouse full of guns, but they took us there blindfolded. Don't know where the fuck it is. But we knew the Bloods'd knocked over the arsenal and—"

Kurtz did not give a shit about the history of Malcolm's weapons heist. He moved the muzzle to Warren's temple and pressed harder. "What did—"

At that instant, the radio squawked in Andrew's voice. "Warren? Douglas? Darren? Y'all all right?" Kurtz turned his head slightly and Warren lunged upward, throwing Kurtz off balance, clambering to his hands and knees.

Kurtz staggered backward but had enough balance to go to one knee six feet from Warren and to aim the .45.

The huge man was on his feet, staring over Kurtz's shoulder at the bodies just visible in the rising light.

"Don't," Kurtz whispered, but Warren opened his hands and came on like a grizzly bear.

Kurtz could have gone for a head shot, but he had more questions. He aimed at the center of the man's Kevlar-covered chest and pulled the trigger.

The impact drove the huge man six feet back, staggering, but—amazingly—Warren did not go down. At that range, with this pistol, the impact must have been incredible—the equivalent of Mark McGwire swinging a bat full-force into an unprotected chest—certainly there were broken ribs, but Warren stayed on his feet, arms still swinging. In the brightening light, Kurtz could see the man's eyes wide and enraged. Warren came on again.

Kurtz fired twice. The big man threw his head back and growled like a bear, but he was driven another seven or eight feet back toward the plastic-covered atrium opening.

"Stop," said Kurtz.

Warren came on.

Kurtz fired. Warren staggered back, then came on again as if leaning into a hurricane-force wind.

Kurtz fired again. Another several steps back. The giant was five steps from the edge of the mezzanine, his huge form silhouetted against the brighter plastic tarp of a wall. Saliva and blood sprayed from his open mouth. Warren actually roared.

"Fuck it," said Kurtz and fired twice more, putting both shots high on the Kevlar vest.

Warren was driven backward like a hammered railroad spike. The huge man hit the plastic, staples ripped out, he teetered, fingernails grabbing the sagging tarp, and then he went back and over the ledge, pulling one hundred and twenty square feet of tarp out of its frame and down with him.

Kurtz walked to the edge of the mezzanine to watch the shrouded figure hurtle downward into the darkened atrium, but had to step back as the man far below opened fire with an automatic rifle. Kurtz had time to realize that Andrew was shooting at Warren before the big man hit the concrete.

Andrew screamed and ran out of the atrium.

Kurtz swept up the Colt M4 carbine and jogged down the short access hall to the east wall. He had pried blocks and bricks out of their moorings there, and the result was a sort of gun slit that let him look down on the east entrance to the building and the streets beyond.

The predawn glimmer gave enough light for Kurtz to see Andrew running hell-bent-for-leather toward the wire fence along the east side of the lot. Sighing again, Kurtz lifted the M4 into the open gap in the wall and used the optic sight to pick up the running figure. He took a breath, but before he could squeeze the trigger, there came the pop and rip of automatic-weapons fire, and Andrew was batted down as if a huge, invisible hand had smashed him away.

Kurtz swung the sight toward the line of cars across the street. Movement. Several dark figures behind the vehicles there.

Kurtz could feel his heart pounding. If Malcolm's men came after him now, he was in a bad place. Kurtz never liked Alamo scenarios.

One of the men jogged forward, crawled through a cut in the wire, and came out onto the lot as far as

Andrew's sprawled body. The shooter raised a radio, but it wasn't tuned to the frequency Warren and his pals had been using. The man went back to the line of cars and several men got into the back of an AstroVan parked at the curb.

Kurtz used the telescopic sight to read the license tag.

The van pulled away and drove out of sight.

Kurtz waited at the gun slit for another thirty minutes, until it was light enough to see easily. He listened very carefully, but the icehouse was silent, except for water dripping and the occasional rustle of torn plastic on the mezzanine.

Finally Kurtz dropped the M4, stepped over the bodies of Douglas and Darren on his way to the stairwell, and went down to the sixth floor. He'd left nothing in his little cubby except an old cot—found in a Dumpster—and an untraceable sleeping bag. But he'd been in here without gloves, so there was always the risk of fingerprints and DNA sampling if the cops got too earnest about solving this multiple murder.

Kurtz had been keeping a five-gallon jerrican of gasoline in a closet. Now he poured gas over his sleeping area and the bathroom, dropped the Kimber .45 onto the cot, and lit a match. He hated to give up the .45— he trusted that Doc was telling the truth in saying the weapons were absolutely cold—but there were at least seven depleted slugs in or around Warren's Kevlar vest that Kurtz did not have the time to retrieve.

The heat and flames were intense, but he had little worry that the whole icehouse would burn down. Too much concrete and brick for that. Kurtz also doubted that the bodies would be burned.

Backing away from the flames, Kurtz turned and jogged down the north stairwell to the basement. The tunnel there was closed off by an ancient steel door that was secured by a new chain and Yale padlock. Kurtz had the key.

He came out in another abandoned warehouse half a block away. Kurtz watched the streets for another ten minutes before stepping out onto the sidewalk and walking away quickly from the icehouse.

CHAPTER 27

"Joe, you look terrible."

Kurtz opened one eye as he lay on the sprung couch in their office. Arlene was hanging her coat and setting a stack of folders on her desk. "Where'd you get that terrible army coat? It's about three sizes too big. . . ." She paused and looked at the bundle of straps and optics on her desk. "What on earth is this?"

"Night-vision goggles," said Kurtz. "I forgot that I had them in my pocket until I tried to lie down here."

"And what am I supposed to do with night-vision goggles?"

"Put them in a drawer for now," said Kurtz. "I need to borrow your car."

Arlene sighed. "I don't suppose there's any chance that you'll get it back by lunchtime."

"Not much," said Kurtz.

Arlene tossed him the keys. "If I'd known, I would have packed a lunch."

"There are places in this neighborhood where they serve lunch," said Kurtz. "Why don't you eat around here?"

As if in answer, Arlene turned on the surveillance monitor. It was 8:30 A.M., and already there were half a dozen men in raincoats looking at racks of XXX-rated videos and magazines upstairs.

Kurtz shrugged and went out the back door, making sure that it locked behind him.

While driving on the state road toward Darien Center and Attica, Kurtz listened to the morning news on WNY radio tell of a fire in an old Buffalo icehouse and four bodies found by firefighters, all four men killed in what authorities described as "a gangland-style slaying." Kurtz was never sure what constituted a "gangland-style slaying," but he suspected it did not involve plummeting seven stories with seven .45 slugs embedded in one's Kevlar vest. He turned up the radio.

Authorities had not revealed the identities of the four dead men, but police had announced that all of the military-type weapons recovered had been stolen in the previous summer's Dunkirk arsenal raid and that the Erie County District Attorney's office was now looking into the involvement of several local white-supremicist groups.

Kurtz turned off the radio, stopped at a roadside rest stop, and left the army jacket draped on a bench at a picnic table. If he'd owned a cell phone, he would have called Arlene and told her to get rid of the night-vision goggles. Kurtz had considered using the goggles as a calling card for Malcolm, but now he just wanted to lose them. He made a mental note to take care of that later.

He drove on to Attica. The little town did not seem familiar to him, and the outside of the State Correctional Facility did not make him feel he was coming home; he had almost never seen the town and exterior of the prison during his years there.

It was Wednesday—visiting day. Kurtz knew that it expedited things to have prearranged the visit, but he filled out the forms, waited more than an hour, and then walked down familiar monkey-puke-green echoing corridors through metal detectors and sliding doors, and then was waved to an empty seat on the visitor side of the thick Plexiglas partition. This made his skin prickle a bit, since he had been in this room a few times.

Little Skag came in on the opposite side, saw Kurtz, and almost walked back out. Reluctantly, sullenly, the short, skinny inmate dropped onto his stool and lifted the phone off the hook. The orange jumpsuit made Little Skag's blemished skin seem almost orange in the sick light.

"Kurtz, what the fuck do you want?"

"Hello to you, too, Skag."

"Steve," said Little Skag. His long white fingers were chewed red and raw around the nails. His hands were trembling. He leaned closer and whispered fiercely into the phone. "What the fuck do you want?"

Kurtz smiled as if he were a friend or family member on his monthly visit. "One million dollars in a numbered Cayman account," he said softly.

Little Skag began blinking uncontrollably. He held the phone in both hands. "Have you gone fucking crazy on the outside? Are you out of your fucking mind?"

Kurtz waited.

"Anything else you want, Kurtz? Want to fuck my baby sister?"

"Been there, done that," said Kurtz. "But after you agree to set up the Cayman account through your private lawyer, I *do* need a phone number."

Little Skag's lips were almost as white as his fingers. Eventually he was able to whisper, "Whose?"

Kurtz told him.

Little Skag dropped the phone and ran his spidery fingers through his greasy hair, squeezing his skull as if trying to drive out demons.

Kurtz waited. Eventually, Little Skag picked up the phone. The two looked at each other in silence for a long moment. Kurtz glanced at his watch. Five more minutes of his visiting time.

"If I gave you that fucking number," whispered Little Skag, "I'd be dead in a month. I couldn't even hide in solitary confinement."

Kurtz nodded. "If you don't give me the number now and make arrangements to set up that account, you'll spend the rest of your life in here. You still Billy Joe Krepp's punk?"

Little Skag winced and his hands trembled more fiercely, but he tried to bluster. "There's no way in fucking hell, man, that I'm going to transfer that kind of money to you—"

"I didn't say it was for me," said Kurtz. He explained, speaking softly but quickly. When he was finished, he said, "And you'll need to use your lawyer's back channels to get in touch with the heads of the other New York families. If they don't understand what's going down, this won't work."

Little Skag stared at him. "Why should I trust you, Kurtz?"

"Skag, I'm the only person in the world right now with a vested interest in you surviving and getting out of here," Kurtz said softly. "If you don't believe me, you could call your father or sister or your *consigliere* for help."

Driving back to Buffalo, Kurtz took a detour north to Lockport. The house on Lilly Street looked quiet and locked up, but it was about the time that schools let out, so Kurtz parked across the street and waited. It was trying to snow.

About 4:00 P.M., just as daylight was beginning to ebb, Rachel walked down the street alone. Kurtz had not seen a picture of the girl in years, but he could not mistake her. Rachel had her mother's fair skin and red hair and thin, graceful build. She even walked like her mother. She was alone.

Kurtz watched as the girl went through the gate of the picket fence, fetched the mail from the box, and then reached into her school backpack for a key. A minute after she had entered the house, a light went on in the kitchen on the north side. Kurtz could not see Rachel through the shutters, but he could *feel* her presence in there.

After another moment, he shifted Arlene's car into gear and drove slowly away.

Kurtz had been very careful to make sure that he had not been followed on his trip out to Attica and back, but he had not been paying attention here in Lockport. He did not notice the black Lincoln Town Car with the tinted windows parked half a block south. He did not see the man behind the tinted glass or notice that the man was watching him through binoculars. The black Lincoln did not follow Kurtz when he drove away, but the man watched through the binoculars until he was out of sight.

CHAPTER 28

"Do I get my car back now?" asked Arlene.

"Not quite yet," said Kurtz. "But I'll drive you home and return it later tonight."

Arlene mumbled something. Then she said, "Pearl Wilson returned your call. She said that she'll meet you at the Blue Franklin parking lot at 6:00."

"Damn," said Kurtz. "I didn't want to *meet* with her, just talk to her."

Arlene shrugged, shut off her computer, and walked to the coat hook on the wall. Kurtz noticed a second topcoat there. "What's that?" he said.

Arlene tossed it to him. Kurtz tried it on. It was long, wool, a charcoal gray, with large pockets inside and out. He liked it. The smell told him that its previous owner had been a smoker.

"Since I had to eat lunch around here, I dropped into the Thrift Store down the block," said Arlene. "That army jacket—wherever it went—just wasn't you."

"Thanks," said Kurtz. "Which reminds me, we have to stop by an ATM on the way to your place. Get about five hundred in cash."

"Oh, you opened an account, Joe?"

"Nope." Before they shut off the lights and went out to the car, Kurtz dialed Doc's number. He wasn't sure how he was going to get to Malcolm Kibunte yet, but he knew that once he did, he'd need more than the short-barreled .38.

Doc's answering machine came on the line with the inevitable "I'm sleeping, leave a message," and the beep.

"Doc, this is Joe. Thought I might drop by later to talk about the Bills." Kurtz hung up. That was enough to let Doc know to leave the steel-mill gate open for him.

Pearl Wilson drove a beautiful dove-gray Infiniti Q45. Kurtz got out of the Buick, blinked against the blowing snow, and got in the passenger side of the Infiniti. The new vehicle smelled of leather and long-chain polymer molecules and of Pearl's subtle perfume. She was wearing a soft, expensive dress of the same dove-gray as the car.

"Seneca Social Club," she said, shifting sideways in the driver's seat. "Joe, honey, what on earth are you thinking about?"

"I just knew that you used to sing there years ago," said Kurtz. "I was just curious about the place. We didn't have to meet in person."

"Uh-uh." Pearl shook her head. "You're never *just curious*, Joe, honey. And you *really* don't want to be messing with the Seneca Social Club these days."

Kurtz waited.

"So after you called," she continued, her voice that husky mix of smoke and whiskey and cat purr which never ceased to amaze Kurtz, "I went back down to the Seneca Social Club to look around."

"Goddamn it, Pearl," said Kurtz. "All I wanted from you was an idea about—"

"Don't you dare curse at me," said Pearl, her rich, soft voice shifting to ice and edges.

"Sorry."

"I know what you *wanted*, Joe, honey, but it's been years and years since I was in that place. Used to sing there for King Nathan when he owned the place. It was a little bar then—a real social club. The layout hasn't changed, but those gangbangers have changed everything else."

Kurtz shook his head. The thought of Pearl Wilson walking among those miserable Bloods made him slightly ill.

"Oh, they'd heard of me," said Pearl. "Treated me all right. Of course, that might have been because I had Lark and D. J. along." Lark and D. J., Kurtz knew, were Pearl's two huge bodyguards. "Gave me a tour and everything."

Kurtz had just driven by the place. No windows on the first floor. Barred windows on the second floor.

Alley in back. A yellow Mercedes SLK parked back there. Steel doors. Peepholes. The Bloods inside would have automatic weapons.

"They've turned it into a pool parlor," said Pearl. "A bar and some tables downstairs. A locked door behind the bar that opens to stairs to the second floor. More tables up there and some ratty furniture. Two rooms up there—the big front room with the four tables, and Malcolm Kibunte's office in back. Another heavy door to his office."

"Did you see this Malcolm Kibunte?" Kurtz asked.

Pearl shook her head. "They said he wasn't there. Didn't see that albino psychopath who hangs with him either."

"Cutter?" said Kurtz.

"Yes, that's his name. Rumor is that Cutter is a black-man albino. Otherwise, the Bloods wouldn't put up with him."

Kurtz smiled at that. "Any back way upstairs?" he said.

Pearl nodded. "Little hall to the back door. Three doors. First one is the back stairway. That door locks from the inside as well. Next two doors for 'Studs' and 'Mares.' "

"Cute."

"That's what I said," said Pearl.

"What reason did you use to get in?"

"I said that I used to sing for King Nathan there, Joe, honey, and that I was feeling nostalgic about seeing the place again. The younger Blood didn't know what I was talking about, but one of the older men did, and escorted me through the place. Everything but Kibunte's office." She smiled slightly. "I don't think that you'll get in by saying the same thing, Joe, honey."

"No, I guess not," said Kurtz. "Many people there? Guns?"

Pearl nodded yes to both.

"Women?"

"A few of their 'bitches,'" said Pearl. Her voice showed distaste at the last word. "Not many. Mostly younger bangers. Crackheads."

"You wouldn't happen to know where Malcolm lives?"

Pearl patted his knee. "No one does, Joe, honey. The man just comes into the community, sells crack and heroin and other drugs to the kids there, and the Bloods make him a demi-god. He drives a yellow Mercedes convertible, but somehow no one ever sees where it goes when Malcolm leaves."

Kurtz nodded, thinking about that.

"It's a bad place, Joe, honey," said Pearl. She took his fingers in her soft hand and squeezed. "I would feel much better if you'd promise me that you're not going to have anything to do with the Seneca Social Club."

Kurtz held her hand in both of his, but all he said was, "Thank you, Pearl." He stepped out of the sweet smells of the new Infiniti and walked through blowing snow to his borrowed Buick.

CHAPTER 29

Doc didn't come on guard duty at the steel mill until 11:00 P.M., so Kurtz had some time to kill. He felt tired. The last few days and nights had begun to blend together in his mind.

Using some of the $500 in cash that Arlene had retrieved from the ATM—Kurtz had promised to pay her back by the end of the month—he filled the Buick's gas tank for her. He then went into the Texaco convenience store and bought a Bic cigarette lighter, twenty-five feet of clothesline, and four half-liter Cokes—the only drinks which came in glass bottles. Kurtz emptied the Coke and filled the bottles with gasoline, keeping out of sight of the attendant as he did so. He had gone into the restroom, removed his boxer shorts, and torn them into rags. Now he stuffed those rags into the mouths of the gasoline-filled bottles and carefully set the four bottles into the spare-tire niche in the Buick's trunk. He did not have a real plan yet, but he thought that these things might come in handy when and if he visited the Seneca Social Club.

It was definitely colder without underpants.

The snow was trying to become Buffalo's first November snowstorm, but little was sticking to the streets. Kurtz drove down to the Expressway overpass, parked on a side street, and climbed the concrete grade to Pruno's niche. The cold concrete cubicle was empty. Kurtz remembered another place where the old man used to hang out, so he drove to the main switching yard. It was on his way.

Here part of the highway was elevated over twenty rails, and in the slight shelter of the bridge rose a ramshackle city of packing crates, tin roofs, open fires, and a few lanterns. Diesel locomotives growled and clanked in the wide yards a quarter of a mile beyond the squatters' city. What little skyline Buffalo offered rose beyond the railyards. Kurtz walked down the concrete incline and went from shack to shack.

Pruno was playing chess with Soul Dad. Pruno's gaze was unfocused—he was very high on something—but it did not seem to hurt his game. Soul Dad gestured him in. Kurtz had to duck low to get under the two-by-four-girded construction-plastic threshold.

"Joseph," said Soul Dad extending his hand. "It is good to see you again." Kurtz shook the bald black man's strong hand. Soul Dad was about Pruno's age, but in much better physical shape—he was one of the few homeless whom Kurtz had met who was not an addict or a schizophrenic. Solid, bald, bearded, given to wearing cast-off tweed jackets with a sweater vest over two or three shirts during the winter, Soul Dad had a mellifluous voice, a scholar's wisdom, and—Kurtz had always thought—the saddest eyes on earth.

Pruno looked at him as if Kurtz were an alien life-form that had just teleported into their midst. "Joseph?" The scrawny man looked warmer in the insulated bomber jacket Kurtz had given him. *Sophia Farino's gift to the homeless,* thought Kurtz, and then smiled when he realized that it had been a gift to the homeless when she'd given it to him.

"Pull up a crate, Joseph," rumbled Soul Dad. "We were just approaching the endgame."

"I'll just watch for a while," said Kurtz.

"Nonsense," said Soul Dad. "This game will go on for another day or so. Would you like some coffee?"

As the older man hunkered over a battered hot-plate in the rear of the shack, Kurtz noticed how powerful Soul Dad's back and shoulders and upper arms were under his thin jacket. Kurtz had no idea where they pirated the electricity for the shack, but the hot-plate worked, and Soul Dad had a refurbished laptop computer in the corner near his sleeping bag. Some form of chaos-driven fractal imagery—almost certainly home-programmed—was acting as a screen saver, adding to the glow of the lantern light in the little space.

Soul Dad and Kurtz sipped coffee while Pruno rocked, closing his eyes occasionally, the better to appreciate some interior light show. Soul Dad asked polite questions about Kurtz's last eleven and a half years, and Kurtz tried to answer with some humor. There must have been some wit in his answers, since

Soul Dad's deep laugh was loud enough to bring Pruno out of his reveries.

"Well, to what do we owe the pleasure of this nocturnal visit, Joseph?" Soul Dad asked at last.

Pruno answered for him. "Joseph is tilting against windmills . . . a windmill named Malcolm Kibunte, to be precise."

Soul Dad's thick eyebrows rose. "Malcolm Kibunte is no windmill," he said softly.

"More a murderous sonofabitch," said Kurtz.

Soul Dad nodded. "That and more."

"Satan," said Pruno. "Kibunte is Satan incarnate." Pruno's rheumy eyes tried to focus on Soul Dad. "You're the theologian here. What's the origin of the name 'Satan'? I've forgotten."

"From the Hebrew," said Soul Dad, rooting around in a crate, taking out some bread and fruit. "It means *one who opposes, obstructs, or acts as adversary.* Thus, 'the Adversary.' He moved the chessboard and set some of the food in front of Kurtz. *"Take thou also unto thee wheat, and barley, and beans, and lentils, and millet, and fitches, and put them in one vessel, and make thee bread thereof,"* he intoned in his resonant growl. "Ezekiel 4:9." He broke the bread in a ceremonial manner and handed a piece to Kurtz.

Kurtz knew that twice a week the nearby Buffalo Bakery left an abandoned pickup truck in its parking lot filled with three-day-old bread. The homeless knew the schedule. Kurtz's belly rumbled. He had not eaten all day. He held the battered, steaming tin coffee cup in one hand and accepted the bread.

"Song of Solomon 2:5," continued Soul Dad, setting two overripe apples on the crate in front of Kurtz. *"Comfort me with apples."*

Kurtz had to smile. "The Bible actually has recipes and recommends apples?"

"Absolutely," said Soul Dad. "Leviticus 7:23 is even so modern as to advise, *Eat no manner of fat*—although if I had some bacon, I'd fry it up for us."

Kurtz ate the bread, took a bite of apple, and sipped his scalding coffee. It was one of the best meals he'd ever tasted.

Pruno blinked and said, "Leviticus also advises, *Ye shall eat no manner of blood.* But I think that is what Joseph has in mind when it comes to this Satan, Malcolm."

Soul Dad shook his head. "Malcolm Kibunte is no Satan . . . the white man who provides him with the poison is Satan. Kibunte is Mastema from the lost book, Jubilees. . . ."

Kurtz looked blank.

Pruno cleared his phlegmy throat. "Mastema was the demon who commanded Abraham to kill his own son," he said to Kurtz.

"I thought God did that," said Kurtz.

Soul Dad slowly, sadly shook his head. "No God worth worshiping would do that, Joseph."

"Jubilees is apocryphal," Pruno said to Soul Dad. And then, as if remembering something obvious. *"Diabolos.* Greek for *one who throws something across one's path.* Malcolm Kibunte is *diabolical,* but not Satanic."

Kurtz sipped his coffee. "Pruno sent me a reading list before I went into Attica. I didn't think it was that long a list, but I spent the better part of ten years working on it and didn't finish it."

"Sapientia prima est stultitia caruisee,'" said Pruno. "Horace. 'To have shed stupidity is the beginning of wisdom.' "

"Frederick was always good for self-improvement lists," said Soul Dad, chuckling.

"Who's Frederick?" said Kurtz.

"*I* used to be," said Pruno and closed his eyes again.

Soul Dad was looking at Kurtz. "Joseph, do you know why Malcolm Kibunte is an agent of Satan and why the white man behind Kibunte is Satan himself?"

Kurtz shook his head and took another bite of apple.

"Yaba," said Soul Dad.

The word rang a faint bell for Kurtz, but only a very faint bell. "Is that Hebrew?" he asked.

"No," said Soul Dad, "it's a form of methamphetamine, like speed, only with the punch and addictiveness of heroin. Yaba can be smoked, ingested, or injected. Every orifice becomes a portal to heaven."

"Portal to heaven," repeated Pruno, but it was obvious that he was no longer a part of the conversation.

"A devil drug," said Soul Dad. "A true generation killer."

Yaba. Shooting yaba. That's where Kurtz had heard the name. Some of the younger cons used it. Kurtz had never had much interest in other people's addictions. And there were so many drugs available in prison.

"So Kibunte is dealing yaba?" said Kurtz.

Soul Dad nodded slowly. "He came first with the usual—crack, speed, heroin. The Bloods were the victors in the gang wars of the early nineties, and to the victors belong the spoils. Malcolm Kibunte supplied the spoils. The usual mindkillers at first—crack, meth, speed, angel dust. But within the past eight or nine months, yaba has flowed from the Seneca Social Club to every street corner. The bangers buy it cheap, but then need it soon and often. The price goes up quickly until within a year—or less—the price is death."

"Where does yaba come from?" said Kurtz.

"That's the fascinating part," said Soul Dad. "It flows in from Asia—from the Golden Triangle—but its use has been limited in the United States. Suddenly here it is in great quantities in Buffalo, of all places."

"The New York Families?" said Kurtz.

Soul Dad opened his large hands. "I think not. The Colombians controlled the drug trade here for decades, but in recent years, the Families have come back onto the scene, working with the Colombians to regulate much of the flow of opium products. The sudden introduction of yaba, although terribly profitable, does not appear to be part of the plan of organized crime."

Kurtz finished the last of his coffee and set the tin cup down. "The Farino family," he said. "Someone in the family is supplying Malcolm. Could it be coming from Vancouver? What source is in Vancouver—" Kurtz stopped in mid-sentence.

Soul Dad nodded.

"Jesus!" whispered Kurtz. "The Triads? They control the flow of junk into North America on the West Coast, and they have plenty of meth labs in Vancouver, but why supply a mob family here? The Triads are at war with the West Coast Families. . . ."

Kurtz was silent for several minutes, thinking. Somewhere in the shack city, an old man began coughing uncontrollably and then fell silent. Finally Kurtz said, "Christ. The Dunkirk Arsenal thing."

"I think you are right, Joseph," Soul Dad rumbled. Closing his eyes, he intoned, *"Our contest is not against flesh and blood, but against powers, against principalities, against the world-rulers of this present darkness, against spiritual forces of evil in heavenly places."* He opened his eyes and showed strong white teeth in a grin. "Ephesians 6:12."

Kurtz was still distracted. "I'm afraid my contest *is* going to be against flesh and blood, as well as against powers and principalities."

"Ahhh," said Soul Dad. "You're going up against the shit-eating Seneca Social Club."

"And I don't have a clue as to how to get to Malcolm Kibunte," said Kurtz.

Pruno opened his eyes. "Which book on my list did you like the most and understand the least, Joseph?"

Kurtz thought a moment. "The first one, I think. *The Iliad.*"

"Perhaps your solution lies in that tale," said Pruno.

Kurtz had to smile. "So if I build a big horse for Malcolm and his boys and seal myself in, they'll wheel me into the Social Club?"

" *'O saculum insipiens et inficetum,'* " said Pruno and did not translate.

Soul Dad sighed. "He's quoting Catullus now. 'O stupid and tasteless age.' When Frederick gets like this,

I am reminded of Terence's comment: *'Ille solus nescit omnia.'* 'Only he is ignorant of everything.' "

"Oh, yes?" said Pruno, his rheumy eyes snapping open and his wild gaze fixing on Soul Dad. *"Nullum scelus rationem habet—"* He pointed at Kurtz. *"Has meus ad metas sudet oportet equus—"*

"Bullshit," responded Soul Dad. " *'Dum abast quod avemus, id exsuperare videtur. Caetera, post aliud, quum contigit, illud, avemus, Et sitis aequa tenet!'* "

Pruno shifted to what sounded like Greek and began shouting.

Soul Dad answered in what had to be Hebrew. Spittle flew.

"Thanks for the dinner and conversation, gentlemen," said Kurtz, standing and moving to the low doorway.

The two men were arguing in what sounded like a totally unknown language now. They had forgotten that Kurtz was there.

Kurtz let himself out.

CHAPTER 30

Kurtz parked next to Doc's old rusted-out pickup with the camper shell on its back. It was starting to snow harder, and the black sky seemed to blend with the looming black buildings. Kurtz put the little .38 in his coat pocket, made sure he had extra boxes of shells in the other outside pocket, and walked across the dark and slippery parking lot into the open maw of the abandoned steel mill.

As soon as Kurtz stepped through the open doors, he felt that something was wrong. Everything looked and smelled the same—cold metal, cold open hearths, huge crucibles hanging like looming soup ladles high above, towering heaps of slag and limerock, a few pools of light from hanging lamps, and the distant glow of Doc's control room thirty feet above everything—but something was definitely wrong. Kurtz's neck prickled and cold currents rippled across his skin.

Instead of walking across the open area between heaps of coal black rock, Kurtz ducked and ran toward a maze of rusted machinery to his right. He slid to a stop behind a low wall of iron, the .38 in his hand.

Nothing. No movement. No sound. Not even a flicker of motion.

Kurtz stayed where he was for a minute, making sure that he was concealed from all sides, catching his breath. He had no idea what had spooked him—but paying attention to such nothings had kept him alive for more than eleven years of prison life, much of that time with a price on his head.

Staying to the shadows, Kurtz began working his way toward the control room. He had briefly considered making a break for the door and then sprinting back to the Buick, but it involved too much open space. If everything was all right and Doc was up there waiting for him, Kurtz might be slightly embarrassed by this melodramatic approach, but he always preferred embarrassment to a bullet in the brain.

Kurtz moved around the edge of the huge space, advancing toward the control room in short sprints of five yards or less, always keeping to cover behind pipes or mazes of I-beams or half-removed machines. He stayed to the ink-black shadows and never exposed himself to fire from darker areas. He made very little noise. This worked for two-thirds of the distance, but when he came to the end of the machinery, he still had sixty or seventy feet of open space between himself and the steel ladder to Doc's control tower.

Kurtz considered shouting for Doc, but quickly decided against it. Even if someone had watched him enter, they probably did not know precisely where he was at the moment. *Unless they have long guns and night-vision goggles like the good old boys in the icehouse.* Kurtz shook that thought out of his head. If they had rifles and scopes, they almost certainly would have taken him when he came through the main doors, still a couple of hundred feet from the control tower.

Who the hell is "they?" thought Kurtz, and then tabled that question for later.

He moved backward, crawling under a latticework of pipes that were each at least a yard across. The metal was inert and empty. Cold seeped up from the concrete floor and made his feet and legs ache. Kurtz ignored it.

Here. Doc's control room was connected to every corner of the huge space by catwalks and here against this brick wall, far from any light, a man ladder ran up to the maze of catwalks.

Kurtz crouched next to the ladder and hesitated. This part of the ladder was cloaked in darkness and shielded from the main space by vertical beams and pipes, but what if the intruders were up on the catwalks, hiding in that very darkness? Or even if they were on the main floor, Kurtz would have to move through relatively lighted areas up there to get to the control room. Despite all the James Bond movies where the secret agent ran across endless catwalks with automatic weapons just kicking up sparks around him, Kurtz knew that there was very little cover on any exposed steel. One aimed slug would probably do the job.

No guts, no glory, said part of his mind.

Where the fuck did that thought come from? replied the sensible majority of his brain. He would do a commonsense audit later.

Kurtz glided up the ladder, his long, dark coat billowing behind him. When he was level with the distant control room, Kurtz threw himself flat on the catwalk, wishing that the steel were solid instead of a grille.

No shots. No movement.

Kurtz moved out from the wall, crawling, his knees and elbows being abraded by the rusty metal, pistol aimed. At the moment, he wished to Christ that he had kept the Kimber .45, incriminating bullet-matches or no. Another reason to get to Doc's control room and supply closet.

At the first juncture of catwalks, Kurtz paused. There was enough metal beneath him and around him here to act as a partial shield for a shot from below, but there were also two tiers of catwalks higher up. Kurtz did not like that. Up near the ceiling, sixty feet above the mill floor, the shadows were almost impenetrable. Anyone already up there would see him silhouetted against the few lights on the floor below, and it was always easier to fire downward with accuracy than up.

Kurtz rolled on his side and studied the approach to the control room.

Three catwalks on this level connected to Doc's glass and steel box, but all three were illuminated from trouble lights below and the glow from Doc's lighted shack. One catwalk ran east and west a dozen or so feet above the control room and connected to this level with a ladder. Twenty feet above that second catwalk, three higher catwalks—and very thin ones at that, as far as Kurtz could tell peering up at the shadows—ran out from the walls to various old crane beams and girders. The highest catwalks crisscrossed above the control tower. This would be the most concealed avenue of approach, and the height—at least sixty feet—might hinder a shot from a handgun. The only problem was that no ladder or stairway ran down from these highest crane-maintenance catwalks to the second level above the control tower. There were a few steel support cables running down, but these looked very thin from this distance.

Fuck it, thought Kurtz and began climbing again.

The high catwalk was half the width of the one he had climbed from. Kurtz's elbows almost slipped over the side as he began crawling out toward the center of the open space. He could feel the narrow catwalk sway to his movement, so he kept his motion as fluid as possible.

It was so damned dark up here that someone could be sitting on the same catwalk ten feet in front of him, and he wouldn't see him. Kurtz thumbed the hammer of the .38 back as he crawled, pistol extended.

Don't be an asshole, came the condescending thought. *Nobody else would be stupid enough to come up this high.*

It *was* high. Kurtz tried not to look down, but it was impossible not to see through the open metal grate of the catwalk. He could see the filthy, littered tops of the floor-level office roofs to his right, the mounds of dark rock heaped like sandbox piles littering the main floor, and the black spiderweb of catwalks and cables below. Kurtz felt a pang of sympathy for the mill workers who would have to crawl out on this exposed, wobbly catwalk to work on the high cranes.

Fuck them. They were probably paid hazardous-duty pay. Halfway out, Kurtz noticed that the catwalk was so unstable primarily because the company had ripped out the crane itself, obviously selling it and its motors and primary support equipment. The catwalks ended thirty feet above and twenty feet beyond the control tower in . . . nothing.

How much support did the crane and its superstructure provide? Kurtz paused and tilted his neck, looking up at where the pitifully few and thin steel cables ended in the ceiling just ten feet or so above him. It was too dark to see cracks or missing bolts, but it was obvious that the cables alone had not been designed to support this catwalk system.

He kept crawling.

Just above the control tower and—despite the shadows—Kurtz began doubting just how invisible he was here. Everything felt exposed and tenuous.

The roof of Doc's control shack was flat and black. The catwalk below looked thin and shaky, and the three catwalks below that were obviously impossibly distant. The only good thing Kurtz could find to think about his present position was that it provided a good vantage point. Nothing moved in the cold, empty space, but much of his field of vision—and fire, if he had been carrying a better pistol or a rifle—was blocked by limerock heaps and hidden by shadows.

Kurtz lay on his side to give his elbows a rest and found that he could feel his heart pounding. Close up, the steel cables he had seen from far away looked even thinner and less substantial than they had from a distance. Each cable was thinner than his little finger, almost certainly was saw-toothed with steel burrs and razor-sharp loose strands, and was attached to the outside of the lower catwalk, making it difficult for him to see how he could even swing over the handrail down there without exposing himself for lethal lengths of time.

I'm wearing gloves, he thought. He flexed his fingers in the thin leather and almost laughed out loud at the thought of the cheap gloves protecting him from steel burrs.

Well, it was either start crawling back toward the wall or do something.

Kurtz thumbed the hammer down, secured the pistol tight in his waistband, swung over the catwalk, grabbed the cable, felt his heart leap into his throat, and then started down as quickly as he could, swaying, using his shoes and hands as brakes, going down hand over hand rather than running the risk of sliding. The control room was thirty feet below and ten feet to his right. There was nothing beneath him except for empty air and cold stone sixty feet down.

Kurtz reached the lower layer of catwalks, swung, missed his first try, and then swung again. He dropped onto the wider catwalk. It swayed, but not as violently as the higher one had.

Not resting for a second, Kurtz loped to the inter-

section of the three walkways, swung over the side to
the man ladder, ignored the rungs, and slid down the
outside rails in pure U.S. Navy fashion.

He hit the lowest catwalk hard, illuminated now by
the glow through the dirty control-room windows just
fifteen feet away. Kurtz rolled, crouched, and moved
in a fast duckwalk to the wall of the control room.

Panting, he moved fast, kicking the unlocked door
open and throwing himself into the room.

Doc's going to laugh his ass off, was his final
thought before hitting and rolling.

Doc was beyond laughing. The old man was lying
in front of the padlocked supply closet. There were at
least four large-caliber entry wounds visible: three on
his chest and one in his throat. Doc had bled out, and
the pool of blood had covered a third of the floor space.
Kurtz swung his little .38 left, right, and left again, but
other than the corpse and him, the control room was
empty.

CHAPTER 31

Kurtz duckwalked closer to Doc's body, keeping his head below the level of the windows, ignoring the blood on his shoes and knees. The padlock to the back room was still secure.

Pistol still covering the doorway, Kurtz patted down Doc's old leather jacket and his bloody trousers.

No keys. Doc kept the padlock keys on a large ring with his other security-guard keys. The key ring was gone.

Kurtz crawled over and checked the desk drawers and even the low filing cabinets, but the keys were gone.

He considered shooting off the padlock, but even as he weighed the pros and cons, he heard footsteps on the floor below. One man. Running.

Shit! Kurtz reached up and turned off the single desk lamp. His eyes adapted quickly, and soon the rectangles of windows and doors seemed very bright. There was no more sound.

Kurtz grabbed Doc by his jacket collar and dragged the old man across the smeared floor. His old acquaintance felt very, very light, and Kurtz wondered idly if it was a result of having bled out.

I'm sorry, Doc, he thought and wrestled the old man to his knees and then upright in the open doorway, using his left arm around the body while he kept to the side of the door, peering around the door frame.

The first bullet hit Doc high in the chest again. The second took off the top of the old man's skull just at the hairline.

Kurtz let the body drop, raised the .38, and squeezed off three shots toward the point of muzzle flash at a bank of machinery about fifty feet away. Bullets whined off steel. Kurtz threw himself back just as four more shots blew out the window on his right and slammed against the open door to his left.

One gun firing, thought Kurtz. *Probably 9mm semi-auto.*

He knew that did not mean that there was only one shooter down there. He doubted if he could be so lucky.

Three more shots, very close together. One came in the open door, ricocheted off the steel ceiling, and struck sparks on the floor and two walls before embedding itself in the desk.

A couple of seconds of silence as the shooter slapped in a new magazine. Kurtz used the intermis-

sion to reload the three bullets he'd fired. His spent
brass rolled into the black pool of blood behind him
and stopped rolling.

Five more shots from below in immediate succession, the loud 9mm blast echoing. Four of the slugs
ricocheted around Kurtz's small place. One of the ric-
ochets slammed into Doc's upturned face with the
sound of a hammer striking a melon. Another ripped
the shoulder padding on Kurtz's topcoat.

This is not a good place, he thought. The shots were
still coming from the heap of girders and dismantled
machinery to the right of the control tower. It was quite
possible—even probable—that a second and third
shooter were waiting somewhere to his left, like duck
hunters in a blind. But Kurtz had little choice.

Swinging into the doorway, he fired all five shots
toward the darkness to his right. The shooter returned
fire—four more shots—the last two ripping the air
where Kurtz had stood only a second earlier.

He ran in the opposite direction along the catwalk,
shaking the spent brass out of the .38's cylinder and
trying to reload as he ran. He dropped a bullet, fumbled
out another. Five in. He snapped the cylinder shut even
as he ran full tilt.

Footsteps pounding below him. The shooter had run
from cover and was running under the control room,
firing as he went. A flashlight beam played along the
catwalk. Sparks leaped and bullets whined ahead of
and behind Kurtz. Could it be just the one shooter?

I couldn't be that lucky.

Kurtz knew that he could never make the extra hundred feet or so to the wall without being hit. Even if

he could, he would be an easy target as he crawled down the ladder.

Kurtz had no intention of running all the way to the wall. Grabbing a suspension cable with his left hand, clinging tight to the .38 with his right, Kurtz swung up and over the handrail and dropped.

It was still a bone-smashing thirty feet to the mill floor, but Kurtz had jumped above the first pile of limerock he had reached, and the heap was at least fifteen feet high. Kurtz hit on the side away from the shooter—smashing into the sharp rock and rolling in a cascade of cinders and stones—but the slope helped break his fall without breaking his neck.

Kurtz rolled out in a landslide of black stone and was on his feet running again before the shooter came around the heap.

Two shots from behind, but Kurtz was already running full speed around the third pile. He slid to a stop and dropped prone, bracing the short-barreled revolver with his left hand clamping his right wrist.

The shooter wasn't coming.

Kurtz opened his mouth wide, trying to calm his panting, listening hard.

Limerock slid and scraped behind him and to the right. Either the shooter or an accomplice was flanking him, climbing over the limerock heap or climbing around it.

Kurtz shifted the .38 to his left hand and rolled right, sweeping black pebbles over him like a man attending to his own burial. He dug his feet into the heap, letting the small, smooth stones slide over him. He butted his head into a depression in the heap and let the black rock cover everything but his eyes. As the stones settled, Kurtz shifted the pistol to his shooting hand, but buried the hand in rock.

He knew that he was only partially covered, quite visible in all but the dimmest light. But the light here was very dim indeed. Kurtz aimed the .38 in the direction of the earlier sound and waited.

Another sliding sound. There was just enough light for Kurtz's eyes to see the silhouette of his attacker's gun arm as it came around the edge of the mound of limerock twenty feet or so away.

Kurtz waited.

A man's head and shoulder appeared and then jerked back out of sight.

Kurtz waited.

The light was stronger behind Kurtz. That meant that the shooter could see silhouettes on the floor or rock pile better than Kurtz could. Kurtz could only wait and hope that he was not presenting a silhouette to view.

The man moved with real speed, coming around the side of the pile and sliding to floor level, weapon raised and braced in the approved style. There was a bulk to the upper body which suggested body armor.

Knowing that any movement would draw fire, but also knowing that he had to change his aim or miss, and thus die in a very few seconds, Kurtz shifted the snub-nosed .38 a bit to the left.

Stones slid.

The man wheeled at the first sound and fired three times. One of the slugs hit a foot or so above Kurtz's right hand and threw stone chips into his face. The second bullet slammed into rock between Kurtz's buried right arm and his body. The third nicked Kurtz's left ear.

Kurtz fired twice, aiming for the man's groin and left leg.

The shooter went down.

Kurtz was up and running toward him, shaking off stones, sliding and almost falling in the resulting rock slide, reaching the shooter just as the groaning man started to raise his weapon again.

Kurtz kicked the 9mm Glock out of Detective Hathaway's right hand, and it went skittering away on cold stone. The cop was fumbling for something with his left hand, and Kurtz almost shot him in the head before he realized that Hathaway was holding up a leather wallet section with his badge catching the dim light. A shield, the cops called it.

Hathaway moaned again and clutched at his left leg with his empty hand. Even in the darkness, Kurtz could see blood pumping from the wound. *Must have nicked the femoral artery.* If he'd hit it full on, Hathaway would be dead by now.

"A tourniquet . . . my belt . . . make a tourniquet," Hathaway was moaning.

Kurtz kept the .38 steady, set his foot on Hathaway's chest—knocking the wind out of him—and held the muzzle a foot from the cop's face. "Shut up!" Kurtz hissed. He was looking over his shoulder, listening.

No footsteps. No noise at all except for the two men's labored breathing.

"Tourniquet . . ." moaned Detective Hathaway, his gold shield still raised like a talisman. He was wearing heavy Kevlar body armor with porcelain plates, military style. It would have stopped an M-16 round, much less Kurtz's .38 slug. But Kurtz's bullet had gone into the cop's leg about four inches below the hem of the vest. "You can't . . . kill . . . a cop, Kurtz," gasped the homicide detective. "Even you aren't . . . that fucking . . . stupid. Tie off . . . my leg."

"All right," said Kurtz, putting more weight on his right foot on Hathaway's chest, but not enough to shut off all breathing. "Just tell me if you're alone."

"Tourniquet . . ." gasped the cop and then gasped again as Kurtz dug his heel in. "Yeah, fuck . . . fuck . . . yeah . . . alone. Let me tie this off. I'm fucking bleeding to death, you miserable fuck."

Kurtz nodded agreement. "I'll help you tie it off. As soon as you tell me why you're doing this. Who are you working for, and how did you know I'd be here?"

Hathaway shook his head. "The precinct knows . . . I'm here. This place will be crawling . . . with cops . . . five minutes. Give me your belt." He held his detective shield higher, his hand shaking.

Kurtz realized that he wasn't going to get an explanation from the wounded man. He took his foot off Hathaway's chest and took a step to the side, aiming the .38 at the detective's forehead.

Hathaway's mouth dropped open—he was breathing raggedly and loudly—and he swung the shield up in front of his face again, holding it in both hands the way someone would hold a crucifix to drive off a vampire. He was gasping, but his voice was very loud in the empty mill, as was the sound of Kurtz clicking the hammer back on the .38.

"Kurtz . . . you fucking *don't kill a cop!*"

"I've already had this discussion," said Kurtz.

In the end, the detective's gold shield was no shield at all.

CHAPTER 32

"Where the fuck is that detective motherfucker?" said Doo-Rag, sitting on the edge of Malcolm's huge desk. "It almost one A.M. Motherfucker should've called by now."

"Get the fuck off my desk," said Malcolm.

Doo-Rag got off, slowly, sullenly, and moved to the leather couch against the wall. He played with the Mac-10 in his hands, clicking the safety on and off repeatedly.

"You click that one more time, motherfucker, and I will have to ask Cutter to re*mon*strate with you, Doo," said Malcolm.

Doo-Rag glared but set the Mac-10 on the couch beside him. "So where *is* the honky cop motherfucker?"

Malcolm shrugged and put his Bally loafers up on the desk. "Maybe Kurtz killed his ass."

"Hathaway that much of a fuckup?" said Doo-Rag.

Malcolm shrugged again.

"How come the cop didn't tell us where this Kurtz motherfucker was going?"

Malcolm smiled. "He probably knew that I'd send you and Cutter and a dozen of the boys to make sure the job was done right and then Hathaway would be out the D-mosque ten Gs."

"But he told us where Kurtz work," said Doo Rag. "That basement under the porn shop. We should be there."

"Nobody there, middle of the night," said Malcolm. "Hold your water, Doo. The cop don't kill Kurtz tonight for some reason, you and your crew can go visit the porn-shop basement tomorrow."

Cutter quit looking out the window and sat on the corner of Malcolm's desk. Malcolm said nothing. Doo-Rag glared at Cutter, then at Malcolm, then at Cutter again. Both men ignored him.

"You really gonna let the honky cop collect the D-mosque's ten grand?" Doo-Rag said after a minute.

Malcolm shrugged. "That's why Hathaway ran the tap on some gun dealer we don't know and didn't tell his cop pals. That's why he went to bust a cap on Kurtz by himself tonight. Nothing I can do if he wants all the money."

Doo-Rag smirked. "You could pop a cap up Hathaway's ass."

Malcolm looked at Cutter and then frowned. "You don't kill a cop, Doo. Only a crazy man would do that."

The three of them were in Malcolm's rear second-floor office. Outside the closed door, in the upstairs pool hall, eight more Bloods were shooting pool or sleeping on couches. Downstairs, there were about twenty more, half of them awake. Everyone was armed.

Malcolm dropped his feet off the desk and walked over to the window. Doo-Rag left his Mac-10 on the couch and came over to stand near him. They were a study in contrasts: Malcolm elegantly dressed and preternaturally still, long fingers quiet, and Doo-Rag quivering and jiving and snapping his twitchy fingers silently. There was not much to see out back: Doo-Rag's red Camaro, Malcolm's Mercedes, a few other cars belonging to the senior Bloods, and a Dumpster. Malcolm had installed a high-output crime light on a pole since his SLK was out there most of the time, but that was a wasted expense. No one was going to steal Malcolm Kibunte's car from the Seneca Social Club.

At that second, Doo-Rag's Camaro burst into flame.

"What the *fuck!??!*" Doo-Rag screamed, achieving an amazing falsetto.

Cutter walked slowly to the window.

Doo-Rag's Camaro was burning steadily, flames leaping from the roof, hood, and trunk. It was obvious that the gas tank had been ignited; but rather than a gigantic, action-movie explosion, it just burned steadily.

"That my *car*, man. I mean, what the *fuck* is going on?" screamed Doo-Rag, hopping around. He ran to the couch and came back with his Mac-10, although no one was in sight in the parking area or alley beyond. "I mean, what the *fuck*?"

"Shut up," said Malcolm. He was poking at his molars with a silver toothpick. He checked out his Mercedes, but it was far from the flames at the opposite end of the lot from the burning Camaro—almost right at the back door—and no one was near it.

Cutter made a sound somewhere between a grunt and a growl. He pointed at the fire and made the sound again.

Malcolm thought a minute and shook his head. "Naww. We won't call nine-one-one yet. Let's see what happen next."

Malcolm's Mercedes exploded in a ball of flame. This time there *was* a movie-style explosion, rattling the caged windows on the second floor with a bone-shaking *whuump*.

"What the *fuck*?" shouted Malcolm Kibunte. "Some bastard fucking with *my* car?" Some of the first-floor Bloods were already out back, milling around with automatic weapons ready, but they were being driven back inside by the heat from the two burning automobiles. Malcolm wheeled on Cutter. "Call nine-one-one. Get the fucking fire trucks here." He pulled his Smith & Wesson Powerport .357 Magnum and ran down the back stairs.

Two fire engines and a fire chief's car arrived less than two minutes later. The big pumper filled the alley, hoses were played out, and more men and hoses appeared down the walkway from the front of the Social Club. Firefighters shouted instructions at one another. The Bloods were also shouting, their weapons visible.

The firefighters backed off. The flames roared.

Malcolm gathered Cutter and a few others around him at the back door. The fire chief, a short, powerfully built man with the name badge HAYJYK on his bulky coat, came up to glare at Malcolm.

"You the asshole in charge here?" demanded Hayjyk.

Malcolm only glared back.

"We've already called the cops, but if you don't get those fucking guns out of here, you're all going to jail and we're going to let that fucking fire burn. And it's about ready to ignite these other four vehicles."

"I'm Malcolm Kibu—" began Malcolm.

"I don't give a fuck *who* you are. You're just another gang punk to me. But get those guns out of sight *now*." Hayjyk was leaning so close to Malcolm that the top of his fire helmet was brushing the taller man's chin.

Malcolm turned and waved his men back into the building. Three police cars pulled up behind the pumper in the alley, their red and white whirling lights adding to the pattern of lights already flickering on all the surrounding buildings.

"Wait a minute," yelled Malcolm, pointing to the four firefighters going in the back door after the Bloods. "They can't go in there."

Hayjyk just grinned without humor, stepped back, and gestured for Malcolm to join him. Malcolm did so, his hand on his .357 Magnum.

Hayjyk pointed up at the roof of the Seneca Social Club. "You're on fire, asshole!"

Malcolm began shoving his way past firefighters, trying to get to the rear staircase. It was locked from the inside. He pushed his way down the hall, Cutter and Doo-Rag shoving aside Bloods and firemen alike.

"You can't go back in there!" shouted Hayjyk.

"Gotta get some papers and shit," said Malcolm, loping up the stairs. The second-floor poolroom was already half-filled with smoke. Firefighters were standing on two of the green felt tables, smashing at the ceiling with their huge axes. The sight made Malcolm sick. Someone had smashed the glass of the rear window in his office, so the space was free of smoke. Malcolm gestured for Doo-Rag to close and lock the door. Then he began pawing papers, guns, and drugs out of the desk and throwing them into a black duffel bag. Luckily, the heroin, crack, yaba, dope, and other drugs were at the arms warehouse out near SUNY. Malcolm had never risked keeping the most incriminating shit anywhere near him. But he had to save his papers and records.

A fireman stepped out of the darkness of the rear stairway. He was carrying an ax backward in his right hand, his left hand was in his coat pocket, and he had a respirator with goggles over most of his face. "You'd be safer outside," said the fireman through his mask.

"Fuck you, man," said Doo-Rag.

The fireman shrugged, took a step forward and clubbed Malcolm over the head with the dull end of the ax. The big man went down heavily. There came two soft *ph-uut* sounds, and Doo-Rag slammed back against the closed office door and fell to the floor. He left a smear of blood on the door.

"Told you it was safer outside," said the firefighter.

Cutter began to move and then froze. A black poly-mer H&K USP .45 Tactical with a silencer was now visible in the firefighter's left hand.

CHAPTER 33

Suddenly someone began pounding on the locked door. A section of ceiling actually collapsed above Malcolm's desk.

Kurtz's gaze shifted for only a second, but the distraction gave Cutter time to flick open a switchblade and lunge for Kurtz's heart. Kurtz had to swing the pistol out of line of fire as he jumped back. Cutter leaped closer. Kurtz brought down the ax while he jumped away, but the ax was heavy and it was clumsy handling it with just one hand. It only deflected the blow. Cutter had the blade swinging again, and he came in fast.

Kurtz dropped the ax, tossed the pistol into his right hand, and tried to bring the H&K to bear, but Cutter had grabbed his right wrist. Kurtz kneed the stocky man in the balls—it didn't seem to have any effect—

and then Cutter's blade was ripping through the left side of Kurtz's heavy coat.

Asbestos and metal fibers sewed into the coat slowed the blade and gave Kurtz a chance to bat away Cutter's right wrist before the knife cut through anything but shirt and skin. Cutter slashed again. Kurtz and Cutter staggered around the room in a clumsy dance, both men breathing hard, Kurtz's plastic mask fogging up. The blade rose and came up fast enough to slash Kurtz's face, but the heavy respirator plastic took the cut. Kurtz tried desperately to free his right hand and the pistol, but the simple truth was that Cutter was stronger than he was.

Cutter's feet came down on Doo-Rag's face; he just dug his boots in for traction. Kurtz slammed into the edge of Malcolm's desk, numbing his thigh. He couldn't see well through the respirator mask, and he didn't have any way to get it off with both hands engaged. Cutter was forcing him back over the desk.

Cutter lunged, trying to gain more leverage for the blade. Instead of fighting the attack, Kurtz went with it. Both men went sprawling, the heavy oxygen tank on Kurtz's back ringing hollowly. The H&K .45 went bouncing across the floor, ending up against Malcolm's arm. Malcolm groaned but did not stir. Smoke was beginning to fill the room and firefighters were shouting in the room next door. The pounding had stopped but someone was chopping at the reinforced door with an ax.

Cutter pivoted the switchblade and slashed the blade across Kurtz's left wrist through the jacket, sending blood spraying.

Kurtz gritted his teeth and threw himself on his back, the oxygen tank ripping at his spine. Cutter lunged, blade swinging.

Kurtz let his heavy firefighter boots take the blows. Cutter pulled the blade back just as Kurtz kicked out once—hard—catching Cutter on the chest and sending him tumbling down the rear stairway and slamming into the door at the bottom. Kurtz had locked the door behind him as he came up the stairs.

Kurtz ripped the mask off. Instead of lunging after the gun and turning his back on the stairway, he pulled the half-liter bottle of gasoline from his coat pocket and lit the short fuse with the cheap Bic lighter. Cutter was already pounding back up the steps.

The Molotov cocktail exploded against Cutter's chest, filling the enclosed stairway with flame and driving Kurtz back from the heat. The office door splintered and gave way. A firefighter's arm appeared, the hand releasing the bolt and turning the knob.

Cutter screamed and tumbled down the steps again, battering at the closed door, trying to get out, but then began climbing the steps again, slowly, inexorably. When the flaming human figure reached the top of the stairs, Kurtz tugged the heavy oxygen tank off his back, handed it to Cutter, and kicked him back down the stairs. Kurtz stepped aside a second before the explosion.

Kurtz picked up the .45, stuck it in his pocket, set his old .38 snub-nose into Doo-Rag's dead hand—it wouldn't pass a paraffin test, but fuck it—swung Malcolm up over his shoulder in a fireman's carry, and got to the doorway just as a real firefighter came into the smoke and confusion. Kurtz pulled the useless respirator back up over his face as more firefighters and cops rushed into the little room.

"Two men down!" Kurtz shouted, pointing to Doo-Rag's corpse and to the flaming rear stairway. The firefighters rushed toward the flame while the two cops knelt next to Doo-Rag.

Kurtz carried Malcolm through the smoky outer room, down the stairs against a tide of shouting firefighters coming up, through the poolroom, out the front door, and past the fire engines and gawking crowd. He avoided the ambulance and the clumps of Bloods being corralled by cops and went down the alley on the opposite side of the street. When he got to the Buick— its trunk already open and waiting—he dropped Malcolm in, took the man's Magnum, and frisked him quickly.

Kurtz slammed the trunk shut and looked around. The Seneca Social Club was in full blaze now, and all attention was focused on it. Kurtz found his .45 and tossed it onto the front seat and then threw the respirator, coat, boots, .357 Magnum, and coveralls into the bushes. Then he got into Arlene's car and drove the opposite way down the alley, coming out on the next boulevard and swinging north.

They had probably already discovered that Doo-Rag had been shot. They would eventually discover one of the responding firefighters tied up and unconscious in the shrubbery near the back alley. It had been Kurtz, of course, who had called 911 a few minutes *before* he lit the gas-doused rags running into the two cars' fuel tanks.

Kurtz noted that despite his dislike of German guns, polymer guns, and silencers, the H&K .45 had worked just fine. It had taken Kurtz just a few minutes after dealing with Hathaway to return to Doc's back room, shoot the lock off, and help himself to the weapons he knew were untraceable.

Kurtz had not gotten the idea for the diversion from *The Iliad*. But Pruno's suggestion of referring to books had reminded Kurtz of a trashy espionage paperback that had made the cellblock rounds at Attica. Something about Ernest Hemingway running around playing spy in Cuba during World War II. There had been a false-alarm fire ploy in that book. Kurtz wasn't proud. He'd steal from the classics some other day.

Wrapping a rag around the bloody but shallow cut on the back of his left wrist, Kurtz drove north.

CHAPTER 34

Niagara Falls is most beautiful in the winter, at night, in a snowstorm. All of these criteria were met as Kurtz parked the Buick—on a side street a few hundred feet away from the American Falls parking lot—retrieved the twenty-five-foot length of clothesline and Malcolm from the trunk, and carried him through a forest of ice-limned trees and snowy fields.

After midnight—it was almost 2:00 A.M.—the powerful searchlights were turned off and both the American and Canadian Falls seemed to roar louder in the darkness. Mist from various cascades drifted across the American-side parks, gathered as ice on the waterfall side of the trees, and occasionally snapped off branches.

Goat Island divided the American Falls from the Canadian, and someone had long since run bridges out to this island and the smaller islands on the Niagara River. The tourist bridges were closed to traffic this night, but Kurtz knew his way through the trees to the bridge and walked out along it, staying near the concrete rail so that his footsteps in the snow would be less visible. At least the heavier snow now would hide his footprints in a few minutes.

Kurtz paused to rest several times. Malcolm was a big man, and nothing is as cumbersome as dead weight. The night was dark, except for reflected light from the low clouds, but the white ripples on the rapids and the blue-white glow at the edge of the American Falls just a hundred yards downstream were quite visible. Malcolm began to stir and moan, but the roar of water masked any noise. Kurtz slogged on, adjusting Malcolm on his shoulder as he got onto the icy walkways of Goat Island and turned toward the observation point near the brink of the smaller Luna Island. The small bridge here rose just a few feet above the raging waters, and Kurtz had to watch his step on the ice. Wooden barriers were set out to keep people away from this point in winter, but Kurtz went around these barriers, coming out from the trees onto the small, icy promontory that separated the broad sweep of the American Falls from the even wider curve of the Horseshoe or Canadian Falls.

Malcolm stirred as Kurtz dumped him at the end of the promontory—less than fifteen feet from the precipice of the Falls on both sides. Kurtz removed Malcolm's billfold. About $6,000 in cash. Kurtz took the money and tossed the wallet in the river. Kurtz was no thief, but he also had no doubt that Malcolm had been paid more than this up front to kill him, so he had little compunction about keeping the money. He tied the end of the clothesline around Malcolm's torso just under the big man's arms and made sure that the knots were firm, even if the rope was cheap. He ran a loop of rope around the icy railing to help act as a brake.

Malcolm began to struggle just as Kurtz manhandled him over the icy railing and dumped him into the Niagara River.

The water revived him and Malcolm began screaming and cursing at the top of his lungs. Kurtz let that go on for a short while—the roar of the Falls drowned out the screams—but, not wanting the man to freeze to death or go over the Falls before they talked, he finally said, "Shut up, Kibunte."

"Kurtz, fuckyouasshole, fuckyouKurtzyouhonky-mother-fuckergoddamn—HEY!!!"

Kurtz had released the rope for an instant, allowing ten more feet to play out, clothesline humming around the railing, stopping it only when Malcolm's feet were five feet from the roaring white foam at the edge of the Falls.

"You going to shut up except when I say talk?" shouted Kurtz.

Malcolm was looking over his shoulder at his legs being tossed out of the water by the violence of the Falls. He nodded wildly. Kurtz hauled him ten feet closer. The two men were only about eight feet apart now—Malcolm's long fingers clawed and grabbed at the icy shore, but slid back into the raging water each time—and they had to shout over the waterfall noise.

"Sorry, they only had cheap clothesline at the Texaco mini-mart," called Kurtz. "Don't know how long it will last. We'd better talk fast."

"Kurtz, goddamn, man. I'll pay money. I've got a couple of million. Money, Kurtz!"

Kurtz shook his head. "Don't need that right now, Kibunte. I'm just curious about who hired you."

"The fucking faggot lawyer. Miles! Miles hired me!"

Kurtz nodded. "But who was behind Miles? Who authorized it?"

Malcolm began shaking his head wildly again. "I don't know, Kurtz. I swear to Christ I don't know. Jesus, it's cold. Pull me in! Money! Cash. I'll take you to it, Kurtz!"

"How much did they pay you for taking me out?"

"Forty K!" screamed Malcolm. "God*damn,* it's cold. Pull me in, Kurtz. Swear to Christ . . . money's yours. All of it."

Kurtz leaned back, holding the terrible weight of the man and the rushing water. The clothesline creaked and stretched. Malcolm shot glances over his shoulder at the blue-white precipice at his heels. Downriver, impossibly far away, car headlights glowed on the arch of the Rainbow Bridge.

"Yaba," Kurtz shouted. "Why yaba?"

"Triad sends it," Malcolm screamed. "Sell on the side. I get ten percent. JesusChristAlmightyKurtz!"

"Ninety percent to the Farinos through the lawyer?" Kurtz shouted over the roar of water.

"Yeah. Please, my man. Jesus Christ! Please. I can't feel my legs. So fucking cold, man. I'll give you all the money . . ."

"And you give the Triad guns from the arsenal raid?" Kurtz called.

"What? Huh? Please, man . . ."

"The guns," Kurtz shouted again. "Triad sends you yaba. You send guns back to Vancouver?"

"Yeah, yeah . . . Jesusfuck!" Malcolm clawed at ice. The current flipped him over and drove him underwater. Kurtz pulled hard and Malcolm's bald head broke through the water again. His collar and chin were crusted with ice.

"How did you kill the accountant?" Kurtz yelled. "Buell Richardson?"

"Who?" Malcolm was screaming now, teeth chattering.

Kurtz let the rope slip three feet. Malcolm clawed at the steep icy shore. His face went under again, and he came up spluttering.

"Cutter! Slit his throat."

"Why?"

"Miles said do it."

"Why?"

"Richardson found the Farino money Miles was laundering—ohSHIIIT!" The current had tugged him another three feet toward the edge.

"Richardson wanted a cut?" Kurtz shouted.

Malcolm was too busy looking at the roaring edge of nothing behind him to answer. The big man's teeth were chattering wildly. He looked back at Kurtz. "Fuck it! You going to let me die anyway," he shouted.

Kurtz shrugged. The rope was cutting into his hands and wrist. "There's always the long shot I'll let you live. Tell me what you know about—"

Suddenly there was a short switchblade in Malcolm's hands. He began cutting through the rope.

"No!" Kurtz shouted. He began pulling.

Malcolm cut the rope, dropped the blade, and began swimming hard. He was a strong, powerful man filled with adrenaline, and for ten seconds or so, it seemed that he was making headway against the wild current—aiming for a point fifteen or twenty feet upriver from Kurtz where he might make a grab for the icy railing.

Then the river reasserted itself, and Malcolm was swept backward as if slapped by the invisible hand of God. He reached the blue-white rim and was swept back and over in an instant—shark-attack fast. It was as if the Falls had swallowed him. The last image Kurtz had of Malcolm was of the man trying to swim into the air, grinning insanely, the diamond stud in his front tooth gleaming in the blue-white glow.

And then there was no one there.

Kurtz pulled the loop of rope free from his bloodless hand and wrist and tossed the remaining length of clothesline into the river. He stood there for only a second longer, listening to the roar of water in the night.

"Should have gone with the long shot," he said softly and turned to leave.

CHAPTER 35

Arlene woke at her usual time—shortly before the gray Buffalo night brightened into gray Buffalo dawn—and was halfway through her morning paper and cup of coffee before she looked out her kitchen window and noticed that her Buick was in the driveway.

She went outside in her bathrobe. The car was locked and the keys were in the mailbox. There was no sign of Joe.

Later, after parking her car and going in through the alley entrance to their basement office, she noticed the white envelope on her tidy desk. Three thousand dollars in cash. November's pay.

Joe came in the back door around noon. His hair had been stylishly razor-cut. He had shaved closely and smelled slightly of an outdoorsy cologne. He was wearing a gray Perry Ellis suit—double-breasted—a white shirt, a conservative green-and-gold patterned tie, and soft, highly polished new brown dress shoes. Joe had always liked the Prince of Wales combination of gray suit and brown shoes, Arlene knew.

"Someone die and leave you money?" she said.

Kurtz smiled. "You might say that."

"How did you get into town from my place this morning?"

"They have these things called taxicabs," said Kurtz.

"You don't see them much in Cheektowaga," said Arlene. "It's more a bus kind of town."

"There are a lot of things one doesn't see much of in Cheektowaga, but I drove to the office just now."

Arlene raised one penciled eyebrow. "Drove? You're driving your own vehicle now?"

"It's a beater," said Kurtz. "An '88 Volvo sedan from Cheaper Charlie's out in Amherst. But it runs."

Arlene had to smile. "I'll never understand your affection for Volvos."

"They're safe," said Kurtz.

"Unlike everything else in your life."

He made a face. "They're boring. And ubiquitous. No one ever paid attention to a Volvo that was following them. They're like Chinamen; they all look alike."

Arlene could not argue with that. She stayed silent while Kurtz carefully removed his jacket and trousers, hung them on hangers on the wall rack, loosened his tie, and lay down on the sprung sofa against the wall. "Wake me about three, would you?" he said. "I've got an important business meeting at four." Kurtz folded his hands on his chest and was snoring softly within a minute.

*   *   *

Arlene tapped the keys and opened file drawers softly,
careful not to wake Joe, but he slept on. She knew that
he would not need the wake-up call—he always awak-
ened exactly when he wanted to—and, sure enough, a
few minutes before 3:00, his eyes snapped open and
he looked around with that instant comprehension
upon awakening, which had always amazed and mys-
tified Arlene.

He dressed quickly, adjusting the suit jacket just so,
buttoning his collar button, and making sure that his
tie was knotted perfectly and that his cuffs shot prop-
erly.

"You need a snap-brim fedora," said Arlene as Joe
headed for the back door, his car keys in his hand. She
did not ask him about the meeting, and he did not offer
any information before he left. Arlene knew from ex-
perience that it might be something as mundane as a
request for a bank loan or something else altogether—
something that Joe might not return from. She never
asked. He almost never told.

Arlene finished a few e-mails to clients and wondered if she should tell Joe that their sweetheart-search
business looked as if it was going to show a profit of
eight or ten thousand dollars by the end of the first
month. She decided to wait.

It was almost 5:00, she was finished with the day's
Web searches and notices, and she was about ready to
call it a day when unusual movement on the small
security monitor caught her eye.

A monster had come in the front door of the porn store. The man's face was half burned away, one eye was swollen shut under inflamed tissue, and only a few white clumps of hair remained on a skull that had been cracked and cooked. The man wore a raincoat open and even through the black-and-white monitor, Arlene could see that his chest was covered with makeshift bandages and raw burns.

The clerk, Tommy, went for the shotgun he kept on the lowest shelf behind the counter.

The monster grabbed Tommy by his ponytail, pulled his head back, and cut his throat from ear to ear with one vicious sweep of his arm.

There were only two customers in the store. One ran for the front door, trying to squeeze past the monster, but the burned man spun quickly and ripped the man from his pubic bone to his throat. The man went down in the entrance and collapsed against the glass counter.

The other customer clutched his dirty magazines to his chest and ran between shelves to hide. The monster followed in three huge steps. The camera showed the mirror in the corner reflecting the monster stabbing downward—three, four, five times.

Arlene's breath had frozen in her chest. Now she lifted the telephone and dialed 911. A voice answered, but Arlene could not speak. She could not tear her eyes from the security-camera monitor.

The monster, raincoat open and bandages flying like a mummy's wrappings, burned face distorted into a snarl, was rushing down the short corridor toward the door to the basement . . . toward her.

CHAPTER 36

Don Farino assembled everyone in the mansion's drawing room. Kurtz had never been in a drawing room—he'd always been amused when he encountered the phrase in books—and was curious about exactly what a drawing room was. After being seated in it, he still didn't know. The room was huge and dark, heavy drapes drawn over deep-set bay windows so that it could have been night for all one could tell from inside, and there were some bookshelves, two large fireplaces—no fires burning—and multiple seating areas scattered around like those in an old hotel lobby. There were six of them in the room, counting the two bodyguards in blazers: Don Farino in his wheelchair next to the black-shaded lamp, Sophia sitting in a plush chair to the don's right, Kurtz on a deep-tufted but uncomfortable leather sofa, and the lawyer, Leonard

Miles, sitting opposite everyone in a straight-backed chair. The two bodyguards stood with their meaty hands clasped over their crotches immediately behind Miles.

Kurtz had been met at the gate and ordered to leave his Volvo parked outside the compound. He wondered if they were afraid of car bombs. The two security goons frisked him very carefully—he'd left the polymer H&K pistol under the front seat—and then drove him up to the big house in a golf cart. The day was cold and gray, and it was getting dark by 4:00 P.M.

The old don greeted Kurtz with a curt nod and waved him to his place on the sofa. Sophia was lovely, wearing a soft blue dress and a smile that was almost— not quite—a smirk. The lawyer Miles seemed nervous.

The four sat in silence for what seemed like a long moment. Kurtz brushed a speck of lint from the crease in his gray trousers. No one offered drinks.

"Have you seen or heard the news today, Mr. Kurtz?" the old man said at last.

Kurtz shook his head.

"It seems that the city's black street gangs and some religious white-supremacist group are at war," Don Farino continued.

Kurtz waited.

"Some anonymous caller informed the white supremacists that four of their members had been killed by some Bloods," continued the old man, his voice sounding raspy but amused. "Someone—perhaps the same caller—informed the Bloods that a rival street gang had started a fire at one of their gathering places. Also this morning, it seems that the police received an anonymous call connecting the death of one of their homicide detectives with the same group of Bloods. So, as the day ends, we have blacks shooting blacks, cops rousting gangbangers, and idiot white supremacists fighting everyone."

After a spell of silence, Kurtz said, "It sounds as if Anonymous has been busy."

"Indeed," said Don Farino.

"Do you give a rat's ass about blacks killing blacks, or whether the Aryan Nation types live or die?" asked Kurtz.

"No," said Don Farino.

Kurtz nodded and waited.

The Mafia patriarch reached down beside his wheel-chair and lifted a small leather valise. When he opened it, Kurtz could see stacks of hundred-dollar bills.

"Fifty thousand dollars," said Don Farino. "As we agreed."

"Plus expenses," said Kurtz.

"Expenses as well." The don closed the bag and set it down. "*If* you have brought us any useful information."

Kurtz gestured with his hand. "What would you like to know?"

The old man's rheumy gray eyes seemed very cold as he squinted at Kurtz. "Who killed our accountant, Buell Richardson, Mr. Kurtz?"

Kurtz smiled and pointed one finger at Leonard Miles. "He did. The lawyer did it."

Miles shot to his feet. "That's a goddamned lie. I've never killed anyone. Why are we listening to this crap when—"

"Sit *down,* Leonard," Don Farino said in flat tones.

The two goons in blazers stepped forward and laid heavy hands on Leonard Miles's shoulders.

The lawyer sat down.

"What evidence do you have, Mr. Kurtz?" asked Don Farino.

Kurtz shrugged. "Malcolm Kibunte, the drug dealer who was hired to kill Richardson, said that Miles had hired him."

Miles was on his feet again. "I've never seen Malcolm Kibunte out of a courtroom where I was defending him. I resent this absurd—"

Farino nodded and the goons stepped forward again. Miles sat down.

"Why would Leonard do this?" Sophia asked in her soft purr.

Kurtz shifted his gaze to her. "Maybe you know."

"What is that supposed to mean?" she said.

"It means that Malcolm and his pal Cutter were the hit men and Miles here was the go-between, but maybe someone else in the family gave Miles the orders."

Sophia smiled pleasantly and shifted so that she was looking at her father. "Mr. Kurtz is crazy, Papa."

Farino said nothing. The old man was rubbing his jaw with one mottled hand. "Why did Miles have Buell Richardson killed, Mr. Kurtz?"

"Your accountant stumbled across quite a few million dollars being laundered through family sources," said Kurtz. "He knew it wasn't from the usual family revenue. He wanted some of it."

Don Farino leaned forward in his chair. "How many million dollars?"

Sophia was still smiling. "Yes, Joe, how many million dollars?" At the use of Kurtz's first name, Don Farino shot a glance at his daughter, but then turned his gaze back in Kurtz's direction.

Kurtz shrugged. "How the hell should I know? Little Skag knew that something weird was going on. That's why he suggested I get in touch with you, Don Farino. He doesn't give a shit about a missing accountant."

Farino blinked. "What are you saying? Why is Stephen interested?"

Kurtz sighed. He wished he was carrying a weapon, but it was too late for that. "Skag started screwing around in the drug business, started sampling his product, and was sent to jail. You and the other families let that happen."

Farino glared. "Mr. Kurtz, it took almost twenty years for the New York State families to come to some accommodation with the Colombians, the Mexicans, the Vietnamese, and all of the other—"

"Yeah, yeah," interrupted Kurtz, "I know all about your little treaties and arrangements and quotas. Who gives a shit? Skag rocked the boat, trying to get more heroin on the streets and money in his pocket, and you let him be sent up for it. But someone using the family contacts opened those floodgates again just a few months ago. Little Skag thinks it's an end run around you, Don Farino."

"He's crazy!" shouted Miles and got to his feet again.

Kurtz looked at the lawyer. "Malcolm Kibunte's gangbangers knocked over the Dunkirk military arsenal last August . . ."

"What has that got to do with anything?" Sophia snapped.

". . . and Miles . . . and whoever's sponsoring Miles . . . has been trading the weapons for yaba and China White and advanced methamphetamine recipes with Vancouver . . ."

"Vancouver?" Don Farino repeated, his tone sincerely puzzled. "Who's in Vancouver?"

"The Triads," said Kurtz. "Malcolm was shipping the guns overland. The drugs came in through the Niagara border checkpoints along with the electronic hand-me-downs from the Vancouver families. Malcolm and his boys knocked over some of the other truck shipments from Florida and New York just to hide what they were really doing. They were just using your family contacts to get the heroin and yaba here, then dumping the junk on the street market, creating a new generation of addicts."

There was a silence. Finally Don Farino stared hard at Leonard Miles. "You traded weapons for drugs with our deadliest enemies?"

"It's a lie." Miles's tone was no longer frightened.

"William." Don Farino, addressed one of the guards. "Charles." To the other man.

The two bodyguards stepped forward and pulled long-barreled .38 revolvers from their shoulder holsters.

"Take Mr. Miles outside and make him talk." The old man sounded very tired. "Then take him somewhere and kill him."

William and Charles stood there, but they did not aim their guns at Leonard Miles. One of the muzzles was pointed at Don Farino and the other at Kurtz.

Leonard Miles had now dropped all of his act of fear and desperation. He showed a particularly nasty grin as he stood between the two guards. "More than one hundred and twenty million dollars," he said in conversational tones. "Right under your nose, old man. Do you think I wouldn't use some of it to buy off everyone on your family payroll?"

Don Farino's head jerked up. Sophia seemed to be meditating. Kurtz sat very still, his palms flat on his thighs.

"William, Charles," said Miles. "Kill the old man and that bastard Kurtz. Here. Now."

Four gunshots roared and the room filled with the stink of cordite and blood.

CHAPTER 37

"Please state the nature of your emergency," said the bored 911 voice.

"There's a madman killing people," said Arlene. She gave the porn shop's address and hung up.

The burned monster was battering the locked door. While the rear door was reinforced by metal, this inner door was just wood. It began to splinter and tear from the hinges as Arlene watched on the small TV monitor.

Arlene grabbed her purse and prepared to run. Which way? Out the back door and she could probably get the Buick unlocked and started before the burned man caught her. Probably.

Through the hidden door into the old parking garage. He wouldn't find the hidden door. *Unless he knew about it.* Then she would be wandering through an empty parking garage with this creature behind her.

The door shook on its hinges. The cheap lock rattled and gave.

He might be after Joe, thought Arlene. *Which means he might come back.*

She had only a few seconds before the madman would be in the basement with her. Arlene grabbed her umbrella from beneath the wall rack and smashed both overhead lightbulbs. Now, with the computer monitor off, the only light came from the small lamp at her desk and the flickering black-and-white security monitor.

Arlene ran back to the desk, switched off the lamp, pushed back her chair, and crouched on one knee. The security monitor showed a static-lashed image of the burned and bandaged monster kicking the door off its hinges.

Arlene turned the monitor off. The long room was suddenly a cave, in near absolute darkness.

Oh God, oh God, I should have put the thing on first. Arlene fumbled in the lower right drawer. She found the heavy goggles, but the straps were too complicated to fit in the dark.

The madman was lurching down the steps. She could hear him—heavy breathing, gasping—she could *smell* him—but she could not *see* him.

Arlene held the night-vision goggles up to her face and fumbled the switch on. Luckily, she had played a bit with the strange thing during her free time. The motor inside the apparatus hummed slightly—and suddenly she could see the basement glowing in green fire.

The madman swung his head in her direction. In this greenish goggle light, his burns and swollen face and hands and sopping bandages were even more terrible. He held a long knife in his right hand. The blade seemed to flicker like a beacon in the amplified night-vision goggles.

The creature was sniffing the air as if searching for her. He began lurching in her direction.

Arlene slid her right hand under the desk drawer, found the hammerless .32 Magnum Ruger revolver there, and lifted the weapon. The goggles slipped in her trembling left hand. Suddenly she was blind.

The burned man ran into the low partition running down the middle of the room. He kicked it to splinters and came on.

My perfume. He smells my perfume.

The creature was ten feet away when Arlene squeezed the Ruger's trigger.

Nothing.

Oh, dear God. I forgot to load it!

The burned man crashed into the far side of Arlene's desk. He swung the knife in a wild arc, hitting the computer monitor and sweeping it and stacks of files off the desk with a crash.

Arlene dropped the night-vision goggles and held the useless Ruger up with both hands. Saliva splattered her as the monster began crawling over the desk. It was screaming obscenities. She could hear him, but not see him.

No, I loaded it. The safety! Once a week a mah-jongg at Bernice's and twice a week to the shooting range since Alan had died.

Arlene clicked off the safety with her forefinger, found the trigger guard, found the trigger, and fired upward into darkness, toward the heat and stench less than a foot above her. She kept firing until the hammer clicked on empty chambers.

CHAPTER 38

The Dane stepped out of the darkness of the draped alcove. The bodyguards, William and Charles, were both down from the double taps. William was still, but Charles was still twitching. Leonard Miles stood in the middle of the emptiness where the two armed men had been. The lawyer was blinking.

The Dane walked over, looked at the twitching Charles, and fired another bullet into the fallen man's head.

Leonard Miles flinched. The Dane pointed one gloved finger at Miles's empty chair. "Sit, please."

Miles sat.

Kurtz was sitting exactly as he had been—feet flat on the floor, palms down on his thighs. Don Farino was holding his chest, but smiling. Sophia Farino had pulled her legs up onto the chair and folded them under her as if a mouse were in the room.

The Dane was wearing a tan-checked wool topcoat, a Bavarian-style hat, dark-rimmed glasses, but no mustache. He walked around and stood behind and to one side of Don Farino. The semiautomatic 9mm Beretta was not precisely aimed at anyone, but the muzzle pointed in the general direction of Leonard Miles.

"Thank you, my friend," said Don Farino.

The Dane nodded.

The don turned his heavy gaze on Miles. "Is my daughter involved in this? Was she the one who gave you the orders?"

Miles's lips were white and trembling. Kurtz saw the yellow silk upholstery on the seat of the upright chair darken as the lawyer urinated in his trousers.

"Speak!" exploded Don Farino. The bark was so loud and fierce that even Kurtz jumped a bit.

"She made me do it, Don Farino," babbled Miles. "She threatened me, threatened to kill me, threatened to kill my lover. She—" He fell into silence the instant that Don Farino made an impatient gesture with his fingers.

The don looked at his daughter. "You traded weapons to the Triads, brought these new drugs into the community?"

Sophia looked at him calmly.

"Answer me you miserable putana!" screamed the don. His face was mottled red and white.

Sophia said nothing.

"I swear to you, Don Farino," Miles babbled, "I didn't want to be involved with this. Sophia was the one who dropped the dime on Stephen. She was the one who ordered Richardson killed. She was—"

Don Farino's gaze never moved from his daughter. "You are the one who turned Stephen in?"

"Sure," Sophia said. "Stevie's a fag and a junkie, Papa. He would have dragged the family down with him."

Don Farino gripped the arms of his wheelchair until his fingers went white. "Sophia . . . you would have had everything. You would have been my heir."

Sophia threw her head back and laughed easily. "Had *everything,* Papa? What is everything? The family is a joke. Its power gone. Its people spread to the wind. I would have had *nothing.* I was only a *woman.* But I want to be *don.*"

Don Farino shook his head sadly.

Leonard Miles took the moment to jump to his feet and run for the door, leaping over the body of William as he ran.

Without raising the Beretta, the Dane shot Miles in the back of the head.

Don Farino had not even looked up. Without raising his head, he said, "You know the price for such betrayal, Sophia."

"I went to Wellesley, Papa," she said. Her legs were still pulled up under her like a little girl's. "I read Machiavelli. If you try to kill the prince, do not miss."

Don Farino sighed heavily. The Dane looked to the old man for instructions. Don Farino nodded.

The Dane lifted the Beretta, swung it slightly, and blew the back of Don Farino's head off.

The old man pitched forward out of the wheelchair. What remained of his face banged into the glass coffee table. Then his body slid sideways onto the carpet.

Sophia looked away with an expression of mild distaste.

Kurtz did not move. The Dane was aiming the Beretta at him now. Kurtz knew that it was a Model 8000 with ten rounds in the magazine. Three were left. The Dane kept a good, professional distance between them. Kurtz could try to rush him, of course, but the Dane could put all three slugs into him before Kurtz could get off the couch.

"Joe, Joe, Joe," said Sophia. "Why did you have to go and fuck everything up?"

Kurtz had no answer to that.

CHAPTER 39

The basement office was overflowing with police and paramedics. Half a dozen of the police were plain-clothes detectives and one of them was a woman with auburn hair. She pulled Arlene aside as the others stood around Cutter's body and talked.

"Mrs. Demarco? I'm Officer O'Toole. I'm Joseph Kurtz's parole officer."

"I thought you were . . . homicide," said Arlene. She was still shaking, even though one of the paramedics had draped a thermal blanket over her after they had checked her out.

Peg O'Toole shook her head. "They just called me because someone knew I'm Mr. Kurtz's P.O. If he was involved with this in any way—"

"He wasn't," Arlene said quickly. "Joe wasn't here. He doesn't even know about this."

Officer O'Toole nodded. "Still, if he was involved, it would go better for him if you and he told us up front."

Arlene had to steady her hand to drink from the Styrofoam cup of water one of the homicide detectives had given her. "No," she said firmly. "Joe wasn't here. Joe had nothing to do with this. I looked on the monitor and saw this . . . this person . . . come in and stab Tommy. Then the man went for the two customers. Then he came down here."

"How did he know there was a basement, Mrs. Demarco?"

"How should I know?" Arlene said. She met the parole officer's gaze.

"Does the name James Walter Heron mean anything to you?"

Arlene shook her head. "Is that . . . his name?"

"Yes," said Officer O'Toole. "Although everyone in town knew him as 'Cutter.' Does that ring a bell?"

Arlene shook her head again.

"And you've never seen him before?"

Arlene put the cup of water down. "I've told about six of the police officers that. I don't know the man. If I've seen him on the street or somewhere . . . well, I don't know him, but how could anyone recognize him with all those terrible burns?"

O'Toole folded her arms. "Do you have any idea where he received those burns?"

Arlene shook her head and looked away.

"I'm sorry, Mrs. Demarco. You do understand that one of those tests the officers performed will tell us if you actually fired the gun."

Arlene looked at her hand and then at the parole

officer. "Good," she said. "Then you'll know that Joe wasn't involved."

"Do you have any idea where we can find Mr. Kurtz?" said Officer O'Toole. "Since this is also his office, we'll have some questions for him."

"No. He said that he had a meeting this afternoon, but I don't know where or with whom."

"But you'll tell him to call us as soon as he checks in with you?"

Arlene nodded.

One of the plainclothes detectives walked over with the night-vision goggles in a plastic bag. "Mrs. Demarco? Could you answer another question, please?"

Arlene waited.

"You say that the assailant was wearing these when he came into the basement?"

"No." Arlene took a breath. "I didn't say that. I told the other officers that the . . . the man . . . took those out of his raincoat pocket and held them up to his eyes."

"Before or after he knocked the lightbulbs out with that umbrella?" asked the officer.

Arlene managed a smile. "There was no other light, Officer. I couldn't very well have seen him take those goggle things out of his pocket if he'd done so *after* he smashed the lights, could I?"

"No, I guess not," said the detective. "But if it was so pitch-dark, how is it that you could see the assailant to fire at him?"

"I *couldn't* see him," Arlene said truthfully. "But I could smell him and hear him . . . and *feel* him as he towered over me." She began shaking again, and Officer O'Toole touched her arm.

The homicide detective handed the night-vision goggles back to an assistant and stood there rubbing his chin.

"I'm sure he wasn't wearing them when I saw him upstairs on the security monitor," Arlene said.

"Yeah," said the male cop. "We've looked at the tape." He looked at Officer O'Toole. "It's part of the Dunkirk arsenal inventory. They just raided a place out by SUNY where Kibunte had a hundred other weapons stored. The Bloods were dipping into them in this war they're having with the white-supremacist assholes. If we hadn't been tipped about this warehouse before the Bloods got there in force, Buffalo would have looked like Beirut on a bad day."

O'Toole nodded, obviously ill at ease speaking in front of Arlene.

"Are you ready to go down to the station with us, Mrs. Demarco?" said the male cop.

Arlene bit her lip. "Am I under arrest?"

The male cop chuckled. "For stopping a piece of shit like this Cutter after he killed at least three people this afternoon? I'll be surprised if the mayor doesn't give you a medal—" He stopped when O'Toole caught his eye. "No, Mrs. Demarco," he said formally, "you're not under arrest at this time. There'll be an investigation, of course, and you'll have to answer a lot of questions tonight and make yourself available to the investigating officers in the coming days, but I'd bet you'd be home by"—he looked at his watch—"oh, eleven at the latest."

"Good," said Arlene. "I want to watch the local news. Maybe *they'll* explain what happened here."

CHAPTER 40

The Dane held the Beretta steady, its muzzle zeroed on Kurtz's chest and never wavering for an instant. Sophia sucked at her thumbnail and seemed to pout. "Joe," she said, "do you have any idea where you are right now?"

Kurtz looked around him. "It looks like the last scene of fucking *Hamlet*," he said.

The Dane's mouth twitched ever so slightly in what might have been a smile.

Sophia dropped her hand from her mouth. "Don't tell me that you've seen *Hamlet*, Joe."

"I see all of Mel Gibson's movies," said Kurtz.

Sophia sighed. "Where you are, Joe, is about half a minute away from being dead."

Kurtz had no comment on that.

"And there's no reason that this had to be the way

things went," she continued. "Why didn't you just let me keep fucking you and leave the rest of this mess alone?"

Kurtz considered not commenting on that either, but finally he said, "Your dad hired me. I had a job to do."

Sophia glanced at her father's corpse and shook her head again. "Some job. Some outcome." She looked at the Dane. "Well, Nils, as I told you on our way to the airport, I hoped it wouldn't come to this—but it has."

Kurtz moved his gaze to the Dane. The man had never relaxed his attention—or the Beretta's aim—for a microsecond. "Nils?" said Kurtz.

"It amuses her to call me that," said the Dane.

"She must be paying you a lot," Kurtz said.

The Dane nodded almost imperceptibly.

Kurtz looked back at Sophia. "One question before the party ends," he said. "Did you hire the homicide cop—Hathaway—to kill me?"

"Sure," Sophia said. She reached into her handbag. Kurtz expected her to pull out a pistol and his stomach tensed, but she raised only a small cassette tape. "Hathaway even brought me the tape of you calling the gun salesperson . . . what was his name? Doc. Hathaway thought I might use it to blackmail you or get your parole revoked, but we decided that a more permanent solution would be better."

"Makes sense," said Kurtz.

"I'm getting bored, Joe," Sophia said. "Your conversation was never very interesting, and today it's deadly dull. Also, we have to call the police and report

this terrible attack by the late Mr. Kurtz at least before
rigor mortis sets in. May I have the Beretta, Nils? I
want to take care of this detail myself."

Kurtz continued sitting the way he had been, but he
was very observant. If there was to be a moment in
which he could act, it would come here.

There was no such moment. The Dane was the con-
summate professional, the muzzle of the Beretta never
wavering even as the Dane moved sideways and
moved the pistol to where Sophia could grasp it with
both hands. When she had it, still aimed at Kurtz's
chest, her finger on the trigger, the Dane took a step
back out of the lamplight and out of any line of fire.

"Any last words, Joe?" said Sophia.

Joe thought for a second. "You weren't all that great
in the sack, baby. I've had sexier encounters with a
Hustler magazine and some hand lotion."

The sound of the unsilenced pistol was very loud.
Two shots.

Sophia smirked. Then she dropped the Beretta and
fell forward onto her father's body on the floor.

The Dane pocketed the .22-caliber Beretta Model 21
Bobcat and stepped forward to retrieve the 9mm Beretta from Sophia's limp hand. Kurtz allowed himself
to breathe again when the Dane slipped the larger Beretta into his pocket as well. Kurtz stood up.

The Dane lifted the valise of cash from its place by
Don Farino's wheelchair and then picked up the small
audiocassette from Sophia's empty chair. "These are
both yours, I believe," said the Dane.

"Are they?" Kurtz asked.

The Dane dropped the cassette into the valise and handed the valise to Kurtz. "Yes. I am a hired assassin, not a thief."

Kurtz took the bag and the two men walked out of the drawing room, Kurtz pausing at the door a second to look back at the five bodies on the floor.

"The last scene of *Hamlet*," said the Dane. "I rather liked that."

The two talked shop as they walked out of the quiet mansion and down the driveway to Kurtz's car.

"You like Berettas?" asked Kurtz.

"They have never disappointed me," said the Dane.

Kurtz nodded. Probably the silliest and most sentimental thing he'd ever done had involved his old Beretta many years earlier.

They had passed the bodies of two guards in the foyer and another—dressed in black tactical gear—was lying outside near the drive.

"Extra work for you?" asked Kurtz.

"I thought it wiser on my way in to see to any possible problems that might hinder our way out," said the Dane. They passed a bush from which two dark legs and a polished pair of loafers protruded.

"Three," Kurtz said.

"Seven counting the night maid and the butler."

"Paid for by someone?"

The Dane shook his head. "I count it as part of overhead. Although the Gonzaga contribution could be prorated toward them."

"I'm glad the Gonzagas came through," said Kurtz.

"I am sure you are." They came to the gate. It had been left open. The Dane put his hand in his topcoat pocket, and Kurtz tensed.

The Dane removed his gloved hand and shook his head. "You have nothing to worry about from me, Mr. Kurtz. Our arrangement was explicit. Despite rumors to the contrary, one million dollars is quite generous, even in this profession. And even this profession has its code of ethics."

"You know the money came from Little Skag," said Kurtz.

"Of course I do. It makes no difference. You were the one who contacted me on the telephone. The contract is between *us.*"

Kurtz looked around. "I was a little worried that one of the Farinos might have outbid me."

The Dane shook his head again. "They were notoriously cheap." He lifted his face to the evening air. It was quite dark now and raining very softly. "I know what you're thinking, Mr. Kurtz," said the Dane. "*I've seen his face.* You haven't. This face is no more mine than Nils is my name."

"Actually," said Kurtz, hefting the valise higher, "I was thinking about this money and what I was going to do with it."

The Dane smiled very slightly. "Fifty thousand dollars. Was it worth all of your aggravation, Mr. Kurtz?"

"Yeah," said Kurtz. "It was." They walked out through the gate and Kurtz hesitated by the Volvo, jingling the keys in his free hand. He would feel better when he had the H&K in his hand. "One question," he said. "Or maybe it isn't a question."

The Dane waited.

"Little Skag . . . Stevie Farino . . . he's going to get out and take over this mess."

"It was my understanding," said the Dane, "that this was what the one million dollars was all about."

"Yeah," said Kurtz. "Little Skag is as penny-pinching as the rest of the family, but this was his one shot at getting back in the driver's seat. But what I meant was that Skag will probably want to tidy up all the loose ends."

The Dane nodded.

"Hell," said Kurtz. "Never mind. If we meet again, we meet again." He got into the Volvo. The Dane remained standing near the car. No bomb. Kurtz started the engine, backed into the empty road, and glanced into his rearview mirror.

The Dane was gone.

Kurtz pulled his pistol out from under the seat and set it on his lap anyway. He put the car in gear and drove away with one hand touching the valise on the passenger seat. Kurtz drove at or under the speed limit. He had no driver's license, and this would be a bad time to be stopped by the Orchard Park sheriff.

He'd driven less than two miles when a cell phone rang in his backseat.

CHAPTER 41

Kurtz slid the Volvo to a stop on a grassy berm and was out the door, rolling in the grass. He didn't own a cell phone.

The phone kept ringing.

Semtex, thought Kurtz. *C4*. The Israelis and Palestinians had specialized in telephone bombs.

Fuck, thought Kurtz. *The money.* He went back to the car, removed the valise, and set it a safe distance from the vehicle.

The phone kept ringing. Kurtz realized that he was pointing his H&K .45 at a cell phone.

What the hell is wrong with me? He retrieved the valise, slid the pistol into his suit pocket, picked up the phone, and hit the answer button.

"Kurtz?"

A man's voice. He didn't recognize it.

"Kurtz?"

He listened.

"Kurtz, I'm sitting outside a little house in Lockport. I can see the little girl through the window. In about ten seconds, I'm going to knock on the door, kill that fucker who's pretending to be her father, and take the teenaged bitch out and have a little fun with her. Goodbye, Kurtz." The man hung up.

Normally it would have been a thirty-minute drive from Orchard Park to Lockport. Kurtz made it in ten minutes, doing well over a hundred on I-90 and almost that speed on the Lockport streets.

He slid the Volvo to a screeching stop in front of Rachel's house.

The gate to the picket fence was open.

Kurtz jumped the fence, .45 raised and ready. The front door was closed. The lights were out on the first floor. Kurtz decided to go in the back way. He moved around the side of the house—not quite running, paying attention but still in a hurry, his heart pounding wildly.

One of the goddamned bushes rose up as he passed.

Kurtz swung the .45 to bear, but too late—a man's arm from the bushes, some sort of camouflage suit, something black and stubby in the man's right hand.

A great, hot force exploded against Kurtz's chest and God's flashbulbs went off in his skull.

CHAPTER 42

Pain.

Good. He was alive.

Kurtz came back to consciousness slowly, very painfully, muscle by muscle. His eyes were open and there was no blindfold, but he could see nothing. He was in great pain. His body did not respond to commands. He was having problems breathing.

It's all right. I may be hurt bad but I'm alive. I'll kill the fucker and get Rachel free before I die. Kurtz concentrated on forcing breath into his lungs and calming his pounding heart and screaming muscles.

Minutes passed. More minutes. Kurtz slowly became oriented in his body and around it.

He was in the trunk of a car. Big trunk, big car. Lincoln or Cadillac. The car was moving. Kurtz's body wasn't moving. His muscles were alternating between cramps and involuntary spasms. His chest was on fire, he was nauseated, and his skull rang like a Buddhist gong. He'd been shot, but not with bullets. *Stun gun,* thought Kurtz. *Taser. Probably rated about 250,000 volts.* Even as his muscles and nerves came back on line, he found he could barely move. His wrists were manacled or handcuffed behind him, cruelly, and somehow attached to manacles around his ankles.

He was naked. The floor of the trunk was covered with crinkled plastic, like a shower curtain.

Whoever it is had it all planned. Followed me to Farino's. Put the phone in the Volvo. Wanted me, not Rachel. At least Kurtz prayed to whatever dark god that the last was true.

He was not quite blind. Brake lights glowed red every now and then, illuminating the carpeted interior, the plastic, and Kurtz's bare flesh. The car was moving, not just idling, leaning around turns, going somewhere. Not much traffic. The road was wet beneath the radial tires, and the sibilant hum made Kurtz want to go back to sleep.

He hasn't killed me yet. Why? Kurtz could come up with a few possible reasons, none very probable. It occurred to him that he had not seen Cutter die.

The car stopped. Footsteps crunched on gravel. Kurtz closed his eyes.

Fresh air and a light drizzle when the trunk was opened.

"Don't give me that shit," said a man's voice with a slight Brooklyn accent. The man set the Taser against Kurtz's heel. Even with the voltage lowered, it was like having a long, hot wire inserted directly under the flesh. Kurtz spasmed, kicked, lost consciousness for a second or two, and then opened his eyes.

In the red light, looming over Kurtz, a Taser in his left hand and a huge .44 Magnum Ruger Redhawk in his right hand, stood a meaner-looking version of Danny DeVito. "You fake being out again," said Manny Levine, "and I'll shove this stun gun up your hairy ass."

Kurtz kept his eyes open.

"You know why you're still alive, fuckhead?"

Kurtz hated rhetorical questions at the best of times. This wasn't the best of times.

"You're alive because my people value burial," said Levine. "And you're going to lead me to my brother for a real burial before I blow your motherfucking head off." He cocked the heavy .44 Magnum and aimed the long barrel at Kurtz's exposed testicles. "But I don't have any reason to keep you in one piece, fucker. We'll start with these."

"Letchworth," gasped Kurtz. Even if he'd been unmanacled, he couldn't have grabbed for Levine at that moment. His arms and legs were still spasming. He needed time.

"What?"

"Letchworth Park," panted Kurtz. "I buried Sammy near Letchworth."

"Where, cocksucker?" Manny Levine was so enraged that his entire dwarf body was shaking. The long steel barrel shook but the muzzle never moved off target . . . targets.

Kurtz shook his head. Before Manny pulled the trigger, he managed to gasp, "Outside the park . . . off Al-

ternate twenty . . . south of Perry Center . . . in the
woods . . . have to show you."

Letchworth was more than sixty-five miles from
Lockport. It would give Kurtz time to recover control
of his body, clear his head.

Manny Levine's teeth were grinding audibly. He
shook with fury while his finger tightened on the trigger. Finally he lowered the hammer on the big Ruger
and hit Kurtz on the side of the head with the long
barrel, once, twice, three times.

Kurtz felt his scalp rip loose. Blood ran salty into
his eyes and pattered on the plastic liner. *Good. Nothing serious. Probably looks worse than it is. Maybe
it'll satisfy him for now.*

Levine slammed the trunk shut, made a U-turn, and
drove away with Kurtz rocking and bleeding heavily
in back.

CHAPTER 43

Kurtz had little sense of time other than the slight ebbing of pain and the even slighter return of muscle control, but it might have been about an hour later when the big car pulled over. The trunk opened and Kurtz breathed deeply of the cold night air, even though he had been shivering almost uncontrollably during the ride.

"All right," said Manny Levine, "we're south of Perry Center. It's all county roads and gravel roads around here. Where the fuck do we go next?"

"I'll have to sit up front and guide you," said Kurtz.

The dwarf laughed. He had small yellow teeth. "No fucking way, Houdini."

"You want to give your brother a decent burial."

"Yeah," said Levine. "But that's Job Two. Job One is killing your ass, and I'm not going to let sentiment get in the way of that. Where do we go next?"

Kurtz took a second to think and try to flex his arms. He'd found during the ride that his handcuffs and ankle manacles were chained to each other and to something solid behind him.

"Time's up," said Manny Levine. He leaned forward with the Taser. The ugly little stun gun had electrodes about three inches apart. He set those metal studs on either side of Kurtz's right ear and pressed the trigger for an instant.

Kurtz screamed. He had no choice. His vision, already impeded by the loose scalp and dried blood, popped orange, bled red, and faded for a while. When he could see and think again, Levine was grinning down at him.

"Half a mile past County Road 93," gasped Kurtz. "Gravel road. Take it west toward the woods until it stops."

Levine reached down, set the electrodes against Kurtz's testicles, and zapped him again. Kurtz's scream lasted long after Levine had slammed the trunk shut and begun driving again.

Levine slammed the trunk up. Snow fell past him in the red glow of the brake lights. "Ready to show me?" said the dwarf.

Kurtz nodded carefully. Even the slightest movement hurt, but he wanted to look more injured than he was. "Help me out," he croaked. This was Plan A. If he was going to lead, Levine would have to unchain him from whatever bolt held him in and undo his ankle manacles. Perhaps he would have to uncuff him while the miserable midget was close enough to grab. It wasn't much of a plan, but it was the best he'd come up with so far.

"Sure, sure." Levine's voice was amiable. He reached over with the Taser and pressed it into Kurtz's arm.

Flashbulbs. Blackness.

Kurtz came to lying on his side on the frozen earth. He blinked his one good eye, trying to figure out how much time had passed. Not much, he felt.

After Levine had zapped him, he'd obviously dragged Kurtz out of the trunk—not carefully, Kurtz thought, feeling a new broken tooth in the side of his mouth—and reworked the bondage arrangements. Kurtz's hands were cuffed in front of him now. Normally this would be good news, but the cuffs were attached by a chain to ankle manacles in state-prison manner, and a longer, fine-link steel chain—perhaps fifteen feet long—ran to a leather loop in Levine's hand.

Levine was wearing a wool cap with earflaps, a bulky goosedown vest, a small candy-orange rucksack, and one of those night-hiking headsets with a battery-powered miner's lamp attached to colorful straps around his forehead. On a normal person, this would have looked absurd: on this dwarf, it looked strangely obscene. Perhaps it was the Taser in his left hand, the dog chain in his right hand, or the huge Ruger tucked in his belt that dulled the humor of it.

"Get up," said Levine. He touched the Taser to the steel dog chain. Kurtz spasmed, twitched, and almost wet himself.

Levine put the Taser in his down-vest pocket and aimed the Ruger while Kurtz slowly, painfully, got to his knees and then to his feet. He stood swaying. Kurtz could rush Levine, but "rush" would mean shuffling and staggering the ten feet while the dwarf emptied the Ruger into him. Meanwhile, although the frozen ground was free of snow this far from the lake, flakes were beginning to fall through bare branches above. Kurtz began shivering violently and could not stop. He wondered idly if hypothermia was going to kill him before Levine did.

"Let's go." Levine rattled Kurtz's chain.

Kurtz looked around to get his bearings and began shuffling into the dark woods.

CHAPTER 44

"You know that Sammy raped and murdered the woman who was my partner," said Kurtz about fifteen minutes later. They had come into a wide, dark clearing, illuminated only by the beam of the lamp on Manny Levine's head.

"Shut the fuck up." Levine was very careful, never coming closer than ten feet from Kurtz, never letting the chain go taut, and never dropping the aim of the big-bore Magnum.

Kurtz shuffled across the clearing, looked at the huge elm tree at the far side, looked at another tree, crossed to a stump, and looked around again.

"What if I can't find the place?" said Kurtz. "It's been twelve years."

"Then you die here," said Levine.

"What if I remember it was another place?"

"You die here anyway," said Levine.

"What if this is the place?"

"You die here anyway, asshole." Levine sounded bored. "You know that. The only question now, Kurtz, is how you're going to die. I've got six rounds in the cylinder and a whole box of cartridges in my pocket. I can use one or I can use a dozen. Your choice."

Kurtz nodded and crossed to a big tree, looking up at a twisted branch for orientation. "Where's the little girl . . . Rachel?" he said.

Levine showed his teeth. "She's upstairs in her house, all tucked in," said the little man. "She's warm enough, but her legal daddy's pretty cold, lying face-down drunk in that fancy-schmancy kitchen of theirs. But not nearly as cold as her real daddy's going to be in about ten seconds if he doesn't shut the fuck up."

Kurtz shuffled ten paces out from the tree. "Here," he said.

Keeping the Ruger Redhawk leveled, Levine took off his backpack, unzipped it, and tossed Kurtz a stubby but heavy metal object.

Kurtz's frozen fingers fumbled unfolding the thing. A folding shovel—an "entrenching tool," the army called it. It was the closest Kurtz would come to having a weapon in his hand, but it couldn't be used as a weapon in Kurtz's condition unless Manny Levine decided to walk five steps closer and offer his head as a target. Even then, Kurtz knew, he might not have the strength to hurt Levine. And chained and manacled as he was, there was absolutely no chance of throwing the shovel at the dwarf.

"Dig," said Levine.

The ground was frozen and for a few desperate moments, Kurtz was sure that he would not be able to break through the icy crust of old leaves and tight soil. He got on his knees and tried to put his weight behind the small shovel. Then he got the first few divots up and managed to start a small hole.

Levine had tied the end of the chain around a sapling. This allowed his left hand to hold the Taser and tap it on the steel chain from time to time. Kurtz would gasp and fall on his side while his muscles spasmed. Then, without a word, he would get to his knees and continue digging. He was shaking so badly from the cold now that he was afraid that he wouldn't be able to hold the shovel much longer. At least the physical labor offered a simulacrum of warmth.

Thirty minutes later, Kurtz had excavated a trench about three feet long and two and a half feet deep. He'd encountered roots and stones, but nothing else.

"Enough of this shit," said Manny Levine. "I'm freezing my balls off out here. Drop the shovel." He raised the Magnum.

"B-b-burial," Kurtz managed through chattering teeth.

"Fuck it," said Levine. "Sammy'll understand. Drop the fucking shovel out of reach." He cocked the huge double-action revolver.

Kurtz dropped the little shovel at the side of the trench. "Wait," he said. "S-s-something."

Levine stepped closer so the headlight beam illuminated the trench, but he took no chances—standing at least six feet from where Kurtz crouched. The shovel was out of Kurtz's reach. The snow was falling heavily enough to stick on the leaves and black soil in the circle of light.

A bump of black plastic protruded from the black soil.

"Wait, wait," gasped Kurtz, crawling down into the trench and scraping away soil and roots with his shaking hands.

Even in the cold night, after almost twelve years, a faint, loamy whiff of decomposition rose from the trench. Manny Levine took a half step back. His face was contorted with anger. The hammer was still back on the Ruger, the muzzle aimed at Kurtz's head.

Kurtz uncovered the head, shoulders, and chest of a vaguely human shape wrapped in black construction plastic.

"Okay," said Levine, speaking through clenched teeth. "Your job's done, asshole."

Kurtz looked up. He was caked with mud and his own blood and was shaking so hard from the cold that he had to force himself to speak clearly. "It m-m-may not b-be Sammy."

"What the fuck are you talking about? How many stiffs did you bury out here?"

"M-m-maybe it is," Kurtz said through chattering teeth. Without asking permission, he crouched lower and began peeling away the plastic over the shape's face.

The twelve years had been hard on Sammy—his eyes were gone, skin and muscle turned into a blackened leather, lips pulled back far over the teeth, and frozen maggots filled the mouth where his tongue had been—but Kurtz recognized him, so he assumed

Manny could. Kurtz's left hand continued peeling away black plastic around the skull while his right hand went lower, tearing rotted plastic around the chest.

"Fucking enough," said Manny Levine. He took one step closer and aimed the Ruger. "What the fuck is that?"

"Money," said Kurtz.

Levine's finger stayed taut on the trigger, but he lowered the Ruger ever so slightly and peered down into the grave.

Kurtz's right hand had already found and opened the blue steel hardcase where he had left it on Sammy's chest, and now he pulled the bundle out still wrapped in oily rags, clicked off the butterfly safety with his thumb, and squeezed the trigger of his old Beretta five times.

The weapon fired five times.

Manny Levine spun, the Magnum and Taser flew off into the darkness, and the dwarf went down. The headlight illuminated frozen leaves on the forest floor. Goose feathers floated in the cold air.

Still holding the rag-wrapped Beretta, Kurtz grabbed the shovel and crawled over to Levine.

He'd missed once, but two of the nine millimeter slugs had punched into the dwarf's chest, one had caught him in the throat, and one had gone in just under Levine's left cheekbone and taken his ear off on the way out.

The little man's eyes were wide and staring in shock, and he was trying to talk, spitting blood.

"Yeah, I'm surprised, too," said Kurtz. Strengthened by the adrenaline rush he had counted on, Kurtz used the entrenching tool to finish him off and then went through the dwarf's shirt pockets. *Good.* The cell phone was in his shirt pocket and hadn't been hit.

Shaking wildly now, he concentrated on punching out the phone number he'd memorized in Attica.

"Hello? Hello?" Rachel's voice was soft, clear, untroubled, and beautiful.

Kurtz disconnected and dialed Arlene's number.

"Joe," she said, "where are you? The most amazing thing happened at the office today . . ."

"You all r-r-right?" managed Kurtz.

"Yes, but—"

"Then shut up and listen. M-m-meet me in Warsaw, the Texaco at the intersection, as soon as you can."

"Warsaw? The little town on Alternate Route Twenty? Why—"

"Bring a blanket, a first-aid kit, and a sewing kit. And hurry." Kurtz disconnected.

It took a minute of pawing around the corpse to find the handcuff and manacle keys and the car keys. Even the goddamned, perforated, bloody goosedown vest was too small for Kurtz—he could barely pull it on and there was no chance of buttoning it—but he wore it as he dumped Levine, the Magnum, the phone, the backpack, the Taser, and his own Beretta—back in its blue-steel hardcase—back into Sammy's shallow grave and began the cold job of filling in the frozen dirt.

He kept the miner's lamp to see by.

CHAPTER 45

Arlene pulled into the closed and empty Texaco station forty minutes after she'd gotten the phone call. Warsaw was literally a crossroads community, and it was dark this night. Arlene had expected to see Joe's Volvo, but there was only a large, dark Lincoln Town Car parked in the side lot of the Texaco.

Joe Kurtz got out of the Lincoln carrying a dashboard cigarette lighter, fooled around by the big car's gas tank for a few seconds, and began walking toward her in the beams of her Buick's headlights. He was naked, bloody, limping, and smeared with mud. The right side of his scalp hung down in a bloody flap, and one eye was swollen and crusted shut.

Arlene started to get out of the Buick, but at that second the Lincoln Town Car exploded behind Kurtz and began burning wildly. Kurtz did not look back.

He opened the passenger-side door and said, "Blanket."

"What?" said Arlene, staring. He looked even worse with the overhead light of the Buick on him.

Kurtz gestured at the passenger seat. "Spread the blanket. Don't want to get blood on everything."

She unfolded the red plaid blanket she'd grabbed from her window seat, and Kurtz collapsed onto the seat. "Drive," he said. He turned the car's heater on high.

They were a mile or so outside of Warsaw, the burning car still an orange glow in the mirror, when Arlene said, "We've got to get you to a hospital."

Kurtz shook his head. The bloody flap of skin and hair on the side of his head bobbled. "It looks worse than it is. We'll sew it up when we get back to your place."

"*We'll* sew it up?"

"All right," said Kurtz and actually grinned at her through the streaks of blood and mud. "*You'll* sew it up, and I'll drink some of Alan's whiskey."

Arlene drove for a moment in silence. "So we're going to my place?" she said, knowing that Joe would never tell her what had happened this night.

"No," he said. "First we go up to Lockport. My car's there and—I hope—my clothes and a certain leather bag."

"Lockport," Arlene repeated, glancing at him. He was a mess, but seemed calm.

Kurtz nodded, pulled the red plaid blanket around his shoulders, and held the flap of scalp in place with one hand while he turned the car radio on with his

other hand. He tuned it to an all-night blues station.
"So all right," he said when he had Muddy Waters
playing, "tell me about this amazing thing that happened at the office today."

Arlene glanced at him again. "It doesn't seem that
important right now, Joe."

"Tell me anyway," said Kurtz. "We've got a long
drive ahead of us."

Arlene shook her head, but then began telling him
about her afternoon as they drove west toward Buffalo,
the blues playing hard and sad on the radio and the
snow falling softly in their headlight beams.

Turn the page for an exciting excerpt from Dan
Simmons' next Joe Kurtz mystery

HARD FREEZE

Now available from
St. Martin's/Minotaur Paperbacks!

Joe Kurtz knew that someday he would lose focus, that his attention would wander at a crucial minute, that instincts honed in almost twelve years of cell-block survival would fail him, and on that day he would die a violent death.

Not today.

He noticed the old Pontiac Firebird turning behind him and parking at the far side of the lot when he pulled into Ted's Hot Dogs on Sheridan, and when he stepped out, he noticed three men staying in their car as the Pontiac's engine idled. The Firebird's windshield wipers moved the falling snow aside in two black arcs, but Kurtz could see the three men's heads outlined by the lights behind them. It was not yet 6:00 P.M., but full night had fallen in that dark, cold, claustrophobic way that only Buffalo, New York, in February could offer.

Kurtz scooped three rolls of quarters out of the console of his old Volvo, slipped them into the pocket of his peacoat and went into Ted's Hot Dogs. He ordered two dogs with everything except hot sauce, an order of onion rings, and a black coffee, all the while standing where he could watch the Firebird from the corner of his eye. Three men got out, talked for a minute in the falling snow and then dispersed, none of them coming into the brightly lighted restaurant.

Kurtz carried his tray of food to the seating area around behind the long counter of charcoal burners and drink machines and found a booth away from the windows where he could still see out and was in line of sight of all the doors.

It was the Three Stooges.

Kurtz had glimpsed them long enough to make a positive identification. He knew the Stooges' real names but it didn't matter—during the years he had been in Attica with them, everyone had known them only as the Three Stooges. White men, in their thirties, not related except via some sexual ménage à trois that Kurtz didn't want to think about, the Stooges were dirt stupid but crafty in their mean and lethal way. The Stooges had made a career of exercise-yard shank jobs, taking orders from those who couldn't get at their targets for whatever reason and contracting their hits out for pay as low as a few dozen cartons of cigarettes. They were equal-opportunity killers: shanking a black for the Aryan Brotherhood one week, killing a white boy for a black gang the next.

So now Kurtz was out of stir and the Stooges were out of stir and it was his turn to die.

Kurtz ate his hot dogs and considered the problem. First, he had to find out who had ordered the contract on him.

No, scratch that. First he had to deal with the Three Stooges, but in a way that allowed him to find out who had put the contract out. He ate slowly and looked at the logistics of the matter. They weren't promising. Either through blind luck or good intelligence—and Kurtz did not believe in luck—the Stooges had made their move at the only time when Kurtz was not armed. He was on his way home from a visit to his parole officer, and he'd decided that even the Volvo wasn't a good place to hide a weapon. His PO was a tough-assed lady.

So the Stooges had him without a firearm and their specialty was execution in a public place. Kurtz looked around. There were only half a dozen other people sitting in the booths—two old-timers sitting silent and apart, and an exhausted-looking mother with three loud, preschool-age boys. One of the boys looked over at Kurtz and gave him the finger. The mother ate her french fries and pretended not to notice.

Kurtz looked around again. The two front doors opened onto the Sheridan Drive side of the restaurant to the south. Doors on the east and west sides of the brightly lighted dining area opened onto the parking lots. The north wall was empty except for the entrance to the two rest rooms.

If the Stooges came in and started blazing away, Kurtz did not have much recourse except to grab one or more of the civilians to use as a shield and try to get out one of the doors. The drifts were deep out there and it was dark away from the restaurant lights.

Not much of a plan, Joe. Kurtz ate his second hot dog and sipped at his Coke. The odds were that the Stooges would wait outside for him to emerge—not sure if he had seen them—and gun him down in the parking lot. The Stooges weren't afraid of spectators, but this wasn't the exercise yard at Attica; if they came inside to kill him, they'd have to shoot all the witnesses—diners and workers behind the counter included. It seemed excessive even for the Attica, Three Stooges.

The oldest of the three boys two booths over tossed a ketchup-covered french fry at Kurtz. Kurtz smiled and looked at the happy family, wondering whether two of those kids, held high, would offer enough bone and body mass to stop whatever caliber slugs the Stooges would be firing. Probably not.

Too bad. Kurtz lifted one foot at a time onto the seat of the booth, removed his shoes and slid off his socks, balling one inside the other. One of the boys in the nearby booth pointed at Kurtz and started babbling excitedly to his mother, but by the time the sallow-faced woman looked his way, he'd tied the second shoe and was finishing his onion rings. The air felt chilly without socks on.

Keeping his eye on the pale Stooge faces just visible through the falling snow outside, Kurtz brought out each roll of quarters and emptied them into the double-thick sock. When he was finished, he set the ad hoc sap into the pocket of his peacoat. Assuming that the

Stooges were carrying handguns and/or automatic weapons, it wasn't quite a fair fight yet.

A Buffalo police officer came into the dining area carrying his tray of hot dogs. The cop was uniformed, overweight, armed and alone, probably on his way home from a day shift. He looked tired and depressed.

Saved, thought Kurtz with only a little irony.

The cop set his food on a table and went into the rest room. Kurtz waited thirty seconds and then pulled on his gloves and followed.

The officer was at the only urinal and did not turn around as Kurtz entered. Kurtz passed him as if heading for the stall, pulled the homemade blackjack out of his pocket and sapped the cop hard over the head. The officer groaned but went down on both knees. Kurtz sapped him again.

Bending over the cop, he took the long-barreled .38 service revolver, the handcuffs, and the heavy baton from his belt. He removed the cop's hand radio and smashed it underfoot. Then he tugged off the cop's jacket.

The rear window was high up on the wall in the stall, was reinforced with metal mesh and was not designed to be opened. Holding the cop's jacket up to deflect the glass and muffle the sound, Kurtz smashed the glass and pulled the metal grid out of its rusted hinges. Stepping up on the toilet, he squeezed through the small window and dropped into the snow outside, getting to his feet behind the Dumpster.

East side first. Sliding the cop's revolver in his belt, Kurtz went around the back of the restaurant and peered out into the east parking lot. The Stooge called

Curly was pacing back and forth behind the few parked cars, flapping his arms to stay warm. He was carrying a Colt .45 semiauto in one hand. Kurtz waited for Curly to make his turn and then walked silently out behind the short man and clubbed him over the head with the lead-weighted baton. He cuffed Curly with his hands behind his back, left him lying in the snow and walked around the front of the restaurant.

Moe looked up, recognized Kurtz, and started fumbling a weapon out from under his thick goosedown jacket even as he began to run. Kurtz caught up to him and clubbed him down into the snow. He kicked the pistol out of Moe's hand and looked through the glass doors of Ted's Hot Dogs. None of the workers at the empty service counter had noticed anything and the avenue was free of traffic at the moment.

Throwing Moe over his shoulder and pulling the .38 from his belt, the baton dangling from his wrist by its leather strap, Kurtz walked around to the west side of the building.

Larry must have sensed something. He was standing by Kurtz's Volvo and peering anxiously through the windows. He had a Mac-10 in his hands. According to other people Kurtz had known inside, Larry had always sung the praises of serious firepower.

With Moe still on his shoulder, Kurtz raised the .38 and shot Larry three times—body mass, head, and body mass again. The third Stooge went down quickly, the Mac-10 skittering away on ice and ending up under a parked SUV. The shots had been somewhat muffled by the falling snow. No one came to the door or window to check.

Still carrying Moe and dragging Larry's body, Kurtz tossed both men into the back seat of his Volvo, started the car, and drove around to the east side of the parking lot. Curly was moaning and beginning to come to, flopping around listlessly with his hands cuffed behind his back. No one had seen him.

Kurtz stopped the car, got out, lifted Curly, and tossed the moaning Stooge into the back seat with his dead and unconscious pals. He closed Curly's door, went around and unlatched the door behind the driver's position, got in, and drove away down Sheridan to the Youngman Expressway.

The Expressway was slick and icy, but Kurtz got the Volvo up to sixty-five miles per hour before glancing around. Larry's body was slumped up against the cracked-open door, Moe was still unconscious and leaning against Curly, and Curly was playing possum.

Kurtz cocked the service revolver with an audible click. "Open your eyes or I'll shoot you now," he said softly.

Curly's eyes flew open. He opened his mouth to say something.

"Shut up." Kurtz nodded toward Larry. "Kick him out."

The pale ex-con's face paled even further. "JesusfuckingChrist. I can't just—"

"Kick him out," said Kurtz, glancing back at the road and then turning around to aim the .38 at Curly's face.

His wrists handcuffed behind him, Curly shoved Moe aside with his shoulder, lifted his legs, and kicked Larry out the door. He had to kick twice to get him

out. Cold air whirled inside the car. Possibly because
of the storm, traffic on the Youngman was light.

"Who hired you to kill me?" asked Kurtz. "Be careful . . . you don't get many chances at the right answer."

"Jesus Christ," moaned Curly. "No one hired us. I
don't even fucking know who you are. I don't even—"

"Wrong answer," said Kurtz. He nodded at Moe and
then at the open door. Icy pavement was roaring by.

"Jesus Christ, I can't . . . he's still alive . . . listen to
me, please . . ."

The Volvo tried to slide a bit as they came around
a curve on the ice. Keeping one eye on the rearview
mirror, Kurtz corrected the slide, turned back, and
aimed the pistol at Curly's crotch. "Now," he said.

Moe started to gain consciousness as Curly kicked
him across the seat to the open door. The icy air revived Moe enough that the bigger man reached up and
grabbed the seat back and held on for dear life. Curly
glanced at Kurtz's pistol and kicked Moe in the belly
and face with both feet. Moe flew out into the night,
striking the pavement with an audible wet noise.

Curly was panting, almost hyperventilating, as he
looked up at Kurtz's weapon. His legs were up on the
back seat, but he was obviously concocting a way to
kick at Kurtz.

"Move those feet without permission and I put two
into your belly," Kurtz said softly. "Let's try again.
Who hired you? Remember, you don't have any wrong
answers left."

"You're going to shoot me anyway," said Curly. His teeth were chattering in the blast of cold air from the open door.

"No," said Kurtz. "I won't. Not if you tell me the truth. Last chance."

Curly said, "A woman."

Kurtz glanced at the road and then back. That made no sense. The D-Block Mosque still had a $10,000 fatwah out on Kurtz as far as he knew. Little Skag Farino, still in the pen, had several reasons to see Kurtz dead, and Little Skag had always been a cheap son of a bitch, likely to hire skanks like the Stooges. An inner-city Crips gang called the Seneca Social Club had put out the word that Joe Kurtz should die. He had a few other enemies who might hire someone. But a woman?

"Not good enough," said Kurtz. He raised the aim toward Curly's belly.

"No, Jesus Christ, I'm telling the truth! Brunette. Drives a Lexus. Paid five thousand in cash up front— we get another five when she reads about you in the paper. She was the one who told us about you probably not carrying today because of your PO visit. Jesus Christ, Kurtz, you can't just—"

"What's her name?"

Curly shook his head wildly. Curly was bald. "Farino. She didn't say . . . but I'm sure of it . . . she's Little Skag's sister."

"Maria Farino is dead," said Kurtz. He had reason to know.

Curly began shouting, talking so fast that spittle flew. "Not Maria Farino. The other one. The older sister. I seen a family picture once that Skag had in stir. Whatshername, the fucking nun, Agelica, Angela, some fucking wop name—"

"Angelina," said Kurtz.

Curly's mouth twisted. "You're going to shoot me now. I told you the fucking truth, but you're going to—"

"Not necessarily," said Kurtz. It was snowing harder and this part of the Youngman was notorious for black ice, but he got the car up to seventy-five. Kurtz nodded toward the open car door.

Curly's eyes grew wide. "You're fucking joking . . . I can't—"

"You can take one in the head," said Kurtz. "Then I dump you. You can make your move, take a couple in the belly, maybe we crash. Or you can take a chance and tuck and roll. Plus, there's some snow out there. Probably as soft as a goosedown pillow."

Curly's wild eyes went to the door.

"It's your call," said Kurtz. "But you only have five seconds to decide. One. Two—"

Curly screamed something indecipherable, scooched over on the seat, and threw himself out the door.

Kurtz glanced at the mirror. Headlights swerved and spun as cars tried to take evasive action, tangled, bounced over the bundle in the road, and piled up behind Kurtz's Volvo.

He lowered his speed to a more sane forty-five miles per hour and exited at the Kensington Expressway, heading back west toward Buffalo's downtown. Passing Mt. Calvary Cemetery in the dark, Kurtz tossed the cop's pistol and baton out the window.

The snow was getting thicker and falling faster. Kurtz liked Buffalo in the winter. He always had. But this was shaping up to be an especially tough winter.